HURRICANE
WILLS

BY THE SAME AUTHOR

Feather Wars
Spilled Water

HURRICANE WILLS

Sally Grindley

BLOOMSBURY

LONDON BERLIN NEW YORK

First published in Great Britain in 2006 by Bloomsbury Publishing Plc,
36 Soho Square, London, W1D 3QY

This paperback edition first published in 2007

A CIP catalogue record of this book is available from the British Library

ISBN 9 780747 590958

Typeset by Hewer Text UK Ltd, Edinburgh
Printed and bound in Great Britain by Clays Ltd, St Ives Plc

3 5 7 9 10 8 6 4 2

www.sallygrindley.co.uk

FSC
Mixed Sources
Product group from well-managed
forests and other controlled sources
Cert no. SGS-COC-2061
www.fsc.org
© 1996 Forest Stewardship Council

The paper this book is printed on is certified independently in accordance with the rules of the FSC.
It is ancient-forest friendly. The printer holds chain of custody.

With thanks to Terri Passenger, Chartered Educational Psychologist, for her guidance

CHAPTER ONE

There's a hurricane smashing through our house. There's a hurricane smashing, trashing, bashing through our house. CRASH! BANG! WALLOP! The doors are slamming, chairs are falling, cushions flying, feet running, voices shouting, 'STOP! STOP! STOP! STOP!'

I'm hiding in my bedroom. I've barricaded my door. I'm not scared, but I don't want to be caught up in it, and I don't want the hurricane turning my room upside down, inside out.

A hurricane can cause total devastation. It can flatten everything in its path. Can you even begin to imagine that? Now try to imagine living with one. I bet you can't.

There's a hammering on my door now. 'Go away!' I yell. 'Leave me alone.' The hammering is harder, louder. I put my hands over my ears to muffle it. I see the door shifting. I run and lean against it. 'You're not coming in!' I yell. 'Go and take a running jump. Go and take a running jump off a cliff.'

I hear laughter then, and a torrent of words. I don't want to hear them. I press my fingers into my ears to block them out. A heavy kick shudders the door, followed by another.

And then it goes silent. So silent. Pin-drop silent. Is it over? I wait. Not a sound. I wait a few minutes longer, then pull the chair away from the door. I'm about to take hold of the handle, when the door crashes open – WALLOP on to my fist – and a deafening BOO! makes my heart boomerang across my chest. A grinning face shoves itself into mine and shouts, 'GOTCHA!', before it yahoos and giddy-ups all the way down the stairs.

'Why don't you grow up?' I bellow after it. 'Why can't you be normal?' I growl under my breath, nursing my bruised fist.

I hide my book under the bed. There's no point in trying to read now, and I don't want the pages scribbled on. I make my way downstairs into the living room. There are cushions all over the floor. The coffee table is upside down. Mum's favourite photograph of me and my brother is in the fireplace. The glass is broken into hundreds of pieces. Mum is sitting on the sofa and I can see that she has been crying. Wills is cuddled up next to her, but I know she doesn't want him there. Not after what he's done, even if he can't help it.

'Mum's cross with you, Chris,' he says smugly. 'Chris cross Chris cross.'

I look at my mother, who shakes her head dully.

'No, she's not,' I say.

'She is, she is, she is,' insists my brother. 'Cross as cross can be, Chris, because you made all this mess and spilt popcorn all over the kitchen floor and it's all sticky wicky.'

I don't bother to argue. 'Shall I make you a cup of tea, Mum?' I ask.

'That would be nice, thank you,' she sighs.

'It's the least he can do, isn't it, Mum?' says Wills.

My mother doesn't reply. Wills stares at her, right in the eyes, waiting for an answer, then he pulls her arm round him and says, 'I'm sorry, Mum. I didn't mean to do it.' He begins to cry, and so does she, and I feel like joining in.

CHAPTER TWO

My brother has ADD. Mum says it stands for Attention Deficit Disorder. I say it stands for Acts Daft and Dumb, which isn't very clever but it tells it like it is, and you try coming up with something better. Wills is thirteen, eighteen months older than me, but sometimes he acts like he's six years younger. Sometimes he acts like he's only two. Less even! Imagine throwing your food across the room when you're thirteen. You just wouldn't, would you? Not unless you were so, so, so mad with someone that you threw it at them because you couldn't help yourself, but even then you probably wouldn't because you'd be too worried that you'd get what for. Wills doesn't care about getting what-for. He's had what-for so many times, but it doesn't make any difference at all. Mum says it's like water off a duck's back, because most of the time he doesn't seem to notice it, and if he does, he just shakes it off. I don't think he actually likes getting into trouble, but he can't always stop himself, so he ignores the consequences.

The worst thing is that Wills looks older than he is. He's nearly six feet tall, and big too. Not like the rest of us. Mum's five feet nothing and as thin as a goalpost, Dad's only five feet eight and shaped like a skittle, and I'm only just taller than Mum. Wills has a moustache already, though he hates anyone to mention it. Mum says it shows up because he's got dark hair. Dad used to have dark hair too, before it stopped growing, which Dad says was because Wills sent it into shock. My hair's fair like Mum's, and curly too, which is a pain, because Wills takes the mickey out of me and calls me Curly Girly. Anyway, when Wills misbehaves, which is often, people tut even more because they think he's a sixteen-year-old behaving like a two-year-old, rather than a thirteen-year-old behaving like a two-year-old, which is bad enough. It doesn't worry Wills though. He just grins and tuts back. Once, in a supermarket, he picked up a huge, and I mean HUGE, jar of pickled onions and held it up to Mum because he wanted her to buy it. When she said no, he dropped it. I don't know if he did it on purpose, but it smashed to smithereens and pickled onions shot across the floor. I wanted to die of embarrassment, and Mum stood there in horror. Wills thought it was hilarious. He started kicking the onions under the shelves and shouting, 'Goal!', even though Mum told him to stop. Then he grabbed one and shouted, 'Catch!' to me. I missed and it hit an old woman – SPLAT! – in the chest. Everyone tutted and said it was disgraceful behaviour for a boy of Wills's age and that Mum should learn to control her children. Wills just thought it was my fault because I was such a lousy catch. He always blames me.

We can't go to that supermarket any more. Even though Mum apologised, they told her that she and her unruly children weren't welcome, and Mum won't go there again anyway because she says she has her pride. Now we have to go to a supermarket five miles away, and I know Mum isn't very happy about it but she doesn't complain.

Sometimes it makes Mum angry when people say she should learn to control her children. 'What do they know about what I have to deal with?' she says. It makes me angry too, because it's not me causing the trouble and I hate being lumped together with Wills, and also because I know what Mum has to deal with. If other people knew what she had to deal with, they'd think she was amazing. I think she's amazing. So does Dad, because he couldn't deal with it.

'I take my hat off to your mum,' he says. 'She deserves a medal for putting up with what she puts up with and coping like she does.'

I reckon I deserve a medal too, for putting up with what I put up with. I'm the one Wills picks on. I'm the one whose homework he scribbles on. I'm the one whose things he takes without asking.

I'm the one whose bedroom he turns upside down when he's lost something of his own. I'm the one who's made to look a fool at school, in the street, in the shops.

'This is my baby brother,' he'll say. 'Isn't he cute? And he's such a goody-goody.' He'll tickle me under the chin, then thump me hard on the arm, or stamp on my foot, and run off laughing with his horrible friends. Or he'll grab my school-bag and take my work out. 'Look at this,' he'll say to his horrible friends. 'Ten out of ten for spelling. He's so clever, my baby brother.'

I hate Wills when he's like that. Hate him, hate him, HATE HIM. Wish he'd never been born. Wish I didn't have to live with him. You'd feel the same, I bet you.

But sometimes, especially when he's not with his so-called friends, Wills gets all sorry, really sorry, and puts his arm round me and says, 'Sorry, bruv, I didn't mean to,' and stuffs a bag of marshmallows into my hand, or a packet of chewing gum.

'Are you sure they're not poisoned?' I'll say, or, 'You haven't licked them, have you?'

He'll look all hurt then. He's good at looking hurt, and he makes me feel bad because I know sometimes he *is* hurt. He's trying his best to make things up and I'm being all suspicious because it's too easy for him to say sorry and I don't want it to be easy because the sorry is never enough – and neither are the marshmallows or chewing gum.

Wills is good at looking innocent too, even when he's as guilty as a dog that's eaten its master's dinner. He opens his eyes wide, looks around him and says, 'Who me? Course not.' Once he followed me into a shop and dropped a firecracker on the floor. He stood there looking so innocent that everyone thought it was me because I blushed bright red, and it was me they asked to leave.

I wish that didn't happen, the blushing thing. It's always happening to me. I only have to see a policeman and I blush as if I've done something wrong. When Wills picks on me at school I always blush, and that gives his mates something else to laugh at. They call me Tomato Head and Little Miss Ruby. I can feel the blush coming on and I try to make myself think cool, calm thoughts, but it's not easy to stop a blush once it's started. The worst time is when someone in class blows off. I always blush then, even if it's not me, and I have to bend right over my work with my head down so that no one can see my face, in case they think I did it. My friend Jack sits next to me and sometimes he blows off on purpose, just so that he can watch me blush.

Thank goodness Wills isn't in my class. He shouldn't even be in the same school as me. He should have gone to senior school by now, but he's so far behind with his work that he's got to repeat a year. It's not that he's stupid, because he's not. When they made him go for tests because of his behaviour, to see if there was anything wrong with him, they said that he was very bright, but had the concentration of a gnat (that's how Dad put it). The concentration of a gnat and ants in his pants – that's how I put it – because most of the time Wills can't sit still for five minutes. Not even two minutes! No wonder he's so far behind with his work. Mum and Dad and the teachers and the people who did the tests have tried all sorts of cunning plans to get him to concentrate, but it never lasts long because they get tired of making all the effort, especially when they're tired anyway.

So just when I was breathing a sigh of relief that he would be gone from school at last, Mum told me that for his own good they were keeping him back. Great. What about my own good?! At least if he wasn't there I would have been able to spend part of my week in a Wills-free zone.

The only time Wills is quiet, the only time he really concentrates – which just goes to show that he can if he wants – is when he's doing his fossils. He's so quiet then that you wouldn't know he was in the house. He's got the most amazing collection: hundreds of them, and gemstones as well. He spends hours cleaning, labelling, cataloguing and arranging them. If you ask him a question, he can tell you everything about each one of them: how old they are, where they were found, where he got them, what they're worth. Sometimes I wish I had a collection like his, but I wouldn't have the patience to spend all that time organising it. Wills gave me one of his ammonites and a piece of amethyst, but it didn't make me feel like starting a collection myself, and I don't think he'd want me to anyway.

If I were to start a collection, it would have to be something completely different. I've got a mouse, and I once thought it would be cool to have lots of mice, but Dad said NO WAY JOSE, which is what he always says instead of just saying no. I think he had visions of the mice multiplying daily until there were hundreds of them running all over the house, nesting in our armchairs, and breaking into our breakfast cereal. THE GREAT MOUSE INVASION! I call my mouse Muffin, because he escaped once (I think Wills helped him) and ate half a chocolate muffin that was supposed to be for Dad's tea. Dad wasn't very happy, but Mum said it would do his waistline the world of good. I keep Muffin in a cage in my bedroom. I don't know why, but I find it comforting to hear him scuffling around while I go to sleep.

I've thought about collecting stamps or coins,

but I haven't done anything about it, so I suppose I'm not really interested enough. Jack makes and collects model aeroplanes. There's no way I can make model anythings with Wills around, not without putting a million bolts on my bedroom door.

My best thing is reading, and I've got loads of books, but that's not the same as collecting fossils. What's good about reading is that if I get right inside a story, right inside, I completely forget where I am in real life. It's like I'm beamed up out of my room into a different world, where no one can reach me and nothing can touch me, not even Wills. The strange thing is that I think it's the same for Wills with his fossils. When he's wrapped up in his fossils, he doesn't even hear when Mum says it's teatime, and he doesn't even realise when he's missing his favourite programme on the telly. Dad says Wills goes off to another planet (sometimes he says Wills comes from another planet!), and that's what happens to me when I read.

My best place for reading is the library. It's only fifteen minutes' walk from home, and I go there whenever there's a hurricane, unless I think Mum needs me. Sometimes I just go there anyway if I've run out of books, or I just want to be on my own, or I've got homework to do and won't be able to with Wills around. Wills doesn't know I go there. I don't want him to know either. Not likely! Jack says going to the library is a bit of an old-people thing to do, but I bet he'd go there too if it was the only way to get some peace. He says only old people and boffins go to the library, and he says I'm not a boffin because I don't come top of the class in anything, so I must be an old person. I thump him when he says that. He doesn't thump me back because he says that you mustn't thump old people, so I thump him again then, but not hard. He knows why I go there and says he doesn't blame me, though he says you wouldn't catch him in a library for all the burgers in McDonald's. He's mad! I would live in a library if I could have all the burgers in McDonald's. I love them, but Mum says they're bad for us, especially for Wills, and will only let us have them if she's feeling really, really lazy and doesn't want to cook, and that doesn't happen very often. Hardly ever. She insists it's because Dad eats too many burgers that he's turned into a skittle. Dad says it's from sitting at a desk for fifteen years.

It's only small, our library, and there are hardly ever more than two people in it apart from me. When you walk in, you have to go left for the children's books and right for the adult books. In the middle, behind the librarian's desk, is a computer where you can go on to the Internet if you want, and behind that is a shelf of talking books. (I've never heard them say a word.)

The first time I went into the library was when I wanted to get away from Wills and his horrible friends. They were following me down the road and yelling things at me, so I ran round the corner and straight through the library doors. I squatted behind a bookshelf until I heard them going past. When I stood up again, this girl, well, woman really, said, 'Are you looking for anything in particular?'

I felt myself go bright red and I wanted to make a dash for it, but she had this sort of big smiley face, and instead I blurted out, 'Have you got any good adventure stories?'

'It must be your lucky day,' she said. 'I put one of our most popular ones back on the shelf this morning. I'll find it for you before someone else takes it out.'

She led me across to the children's section.

'I haven't seen you in here before, have I?' she asked.

I shook my head and felt guilty because my English teacher was always telling us we should go to the library, but nobody did.

'My name's Penny,' she said. 'I'm the librarian here.'

I didn't know if I was supposed to tell her my name, so I just nodded my head and wondered if being a librarian meant that you got to read all the books in the library, and how long that would take.

'Were those boys who went past annoying you?' she said then.

She spoke really kindly, a bit posh but friendly, and she was quite young. I felt like telling her that one of them was my brother and that he spent his life annoying me, but I just said that they were annoying me a bit and that I could handle it. She looked at me a bit like teachers do sometimes when they think you might be telling porkies, but she just turned to the books and pulled one from a shelf.

'Here you are,' she said. 'It's had rave reviews, and everyone who has borrowed it says it's great. I haven't read it myself, though, so don't shoot me if you hate it.'

So they didn't read all the books, I thought. Then she showed me what I had to do if I wanted to take the book home for a few days, and I thought it was amazing that you could do that, because most of the people I knew would never bring it back.

Anyway, now I go to the library a lot, and Penny's like a friend and I can talk to her about things. I've told her about Wills. She says he must be a nightmare to live with. I feel a bit guilty when she says that because he's my brother, but at least she understands about the peace and quiet, and she doesn't push me to tell her things that I don't want to tell her.

CHAPTER THREE

Dad doesn't live with us any more. He left three months ago. He didn't say it was because of Wills, but I bet it was. Dad just can't cope with him. He tries. He tries really hard. He's not very patient though. He explodes like a volcano. You can just imagine it: Volcano meets Hurricane – WHAM, BAM, POW! – Everything destroyed in their paths, including Mum and me, if we don't dive for cover quickly enough.

When Dad told me he was going, I didn't believe him first of all. I couldn't believe him. I thought he just wouldn't do that to us. Then when I realised he meant it, I begged him to stay. I hugged my arms round his waist, and held on as tightly as I could to try to stop him from going. He stroked my hair and I felt him sort of shudder and I looked up. I'd never seen Dad cry before, and he turned away so that I wouldn't see him then, but I knew that's what he was doing because he wiped a hand across his eyes.

'Don't go, Dad,' I pleaded. 'Please don't go.'

'It'll be all right, Christopher,' he said. 'I won't be going far, just round the corner, so you'll be able to come and see me as often as you like.'

It was like he had cut himself off already when he called me Christopher, because he never calls me Christopher unless he's cross with me.

'Don't you love us any more?' I asked, and he said that of course he did, but that it would be better like this. I couldn't see how it would be better, but Mum came in with Wills then and I didn't have a chance to ask.

Wills went berserk. He screamed and threw himself under the kitchen table and said he wouldn't come out until Dad changed his mind. Mum pleaded with him, and I thought Dad was going to lose his temper but he didn't. He crawled under the table, which is difficult when you're shaped like a skittle, and sat there talking to Wills until he had calmed down. Mum and I looked at each other and sort of smiled – though it wasn't really a smiling matter – because all we could see were four feet sticking out from under the table-cloth. We went and sat in the living room until the storm had blown out. Mum put her arm round me and asked if I was all right. I said that I was, but I didn't really know because Dad hadn't gone yet, and I thought that he might have to stay because of the fuss Wills was making.

When at last they came into the living room, Dad was bright pink and sweating all over the top of his head. Wills had a big grin on his face.

'Dad's going to take us motor racing,' he said.

'When?' I asked, even though I knew what the answer would be.

'When I can sort something out,' said Dad, dropping into an armchair and mopping his fore-head with a handkerchief.

That's typical Dad. He's always making promises. But he's not very good at the sorting-some-thing-out part of it. I don't think he does it on purpose. He just forgets, or he doesn't get round to it, or other things get in the way, or he doesn't know how to make it happen. And sometimes he promises something just to shut me or Wills up. Like then. Except it didn't shut Wills up. Wills began to run round the room making racing-car noises. Mum put her fingers in her ears and frowned at Dad. Dad told Wills to stop, but he kept going, – 'NYEEEAHHH, NYEEEAHHH, NYEEEAHHH' – until Dad stood up and yelled at the top of his voice,

'STOP IT, WILLIAM, NOW!' Volcano meets Hurricane. 'STOP IT THIS MINUTE. DO YOU HEAR ME?'

Wills heard him all right. He stopped in his tracks and glared at Dad.

'You can't tell me what to do,' he hissed. 'You're not my dad any more. You're going away and leaving us.'

'Don't, Wills!' cried Mum. She jumped up from the settee and tried to put her arms round him, but he pushed her away and ran upstairs to his room. Music on LOUD.

Dad looked as if he had been punched in the face. He took a deep breath, squeezed me on the shoulder, kissed Mum on the cheek, then walked out through the door and out of the house.

Wills refused to come down for dinner that evening, even though Mum tried to tempt him with exaggerated descriptions of the lemon meringue pie she had made, which is his favourite apart from jam roly-poly.

'I'm not eating till Dad comes back,' was all he would say.

Mum and I picked at our spaghetti bolognese, listening for his bedroom door to open, and sort of listening for the key in the front door.

'Will Dad ever come back?' I asked Mum.

'Maybe,' she said. 'I don't know, Chris. But try not to blame your father. It's not his fault that he finds it difficult.'

I did blame my father then. He should have been stronger, should have been tougher, should have been able to cope. He was supposed to look after us come what may, not run away because he found it difficult.

'He's made it more difficult for you now, Mum,' I said. 'I can blame him for that.'

'He thinks it'll help, because when you and Wills go to stay with him I'll be able to have a break.'

She tried to tell me then that there were lots of reasons why Dad was leaving and that I wasn't to think it was because of Wills. There were grown-up things that I wouldn't understand. I didn't believe her though. And I could tell from the way she looked so sad that she wanted Dad to be there, volcano or no volcano.

'Maybe he'll miss us so much he'll have to come back,' I urged. Surely he *would* miss us so much he would have to come back. Would he though? What if he found he liked the peace and quiet of his hurricane-free zone?

'You're right,' said Mum brightly. 'Of course he'll miss us.'

I looked at her. She may have sounded bright, but her eyes were sort of dull and I knew that she didn't really believe it.

I couldn't sleep that night. I kept wondering where Dad was and when I would see him again. I wondered if he was thinking about us or whether he had already shut us out of his mind. I wondered how we would manage without him, how Mum would manage without him.

In the middle of the night, I heard Wills's door open. I heard him go downstairs into the kitchen and raid the fridge. I must have dropped off asleep, because I didn't hear him come back upstairs again.

I was startled by a light joggling across my eyes.

'Chris – are you awake?'

'What the hell are you doing, Wills? You frightened the pants off me. What time is it?'

I heaved myself up against the pillows. Wills sat down on the bed and laid his torch on his lap.

'It's three o'clock,' he whispered. 'Dad hasn't come back yet.'

'He's not coming back, Wills, he told you that. Not for the moment, anyway.'

'Bastard,' spat Wills. He chewed at the inside of his mouth, then moved on to his fingernails.

'We'll still be able to see him,' I said. 'Just not every day.'

'I don't want to see him ever again,' Wills hissed. 'Never, never, never.'

'Don't be daft,' I said. 'He's our dad.'

'Was our dad,' said Wills.

I didn't want to hear him say that again. 'Go back to your room, Wills,' I ordered. 'I want to go to sleep.'

Wills hesitated, then whispered, 'Do you wanna see something?'

Before I could answer, he jumped up from the bed, went into his own room, and came back, clutching something big and round.

'What is it?' I asked.

'It's an ammonite. Look, it's a perfect round. No bits missing, no chips, nothing.'

I took it from him and looked at it. It was bigger than the whole of my hand. I traced the swirls with my finger, before Wills grabbed it back.

'Where d'you get it?' I asked.

'None of your business,' he said sharply. He turned and ran his fingers across the bars of

Muffin's cage. Then, 'A friend gave it to me,' he said. 'It's cool, isn't it? It's the best one I've got.'

I could tell Wills was lying. He had this look about him. Then he said, 'Don't tell Mum about it, will you? She'll think I stole it, but I didn't.'

I didn't know what to say then. I was sure Wills was lying, but I didn't think he would steal something.

'Promise you won't tell Mum,' he insisted.

'I wish you hadn't shown it to me now,' I retorted. 'I promise, now let me get some sleep, will you?'

'*I* wish I hadn't shown you, misery guts,' fired Wills.

He sloped off back to his room, leaving me to wonder why he couldn't have kept his ammonite to himself, especially since he didn't want Mum to know that he'd got it. I supposed it must be that he couldn't keep it to himself, because there was no point in having something precious if no one else knew about it. I always told Mum or Dad if I'd read a really good book, or got ten out of ten, and I always wanted them to be watching if I came first in a race or scored a good goal, which didn't happen very often. That was the same thing really as Wills wanting to show off his ammonite, except that he'd chosen to show me and not Mum. And Dad wasn't there now.

I couldn't get back to sleep after that. Muffin had woken up and was spinning round on his wheel. The rattling got into my head. I lay there, hoping that Wills wouldn't tell me anything else he didn't want Mum to know. I didn't want to know things that I wasn't supposed to tell her.

The next day was a Saturday, which made it worse that Dad wasn't there. Dad always did a fry-up on Saturdays and Sundays. It was his weekend treat since he didn't have to go to work. Mum cooked the fry-up instead, but it wasn't the same. With Dad, we would sit at the kitchen table and he would read bits out of the newspaper in between slurps of tea. He's good at finding the funny bits, like the story about a man who was sent to prison because he kept stealing cars in order to clean them, and the one about a boy who wrote in an exam that you can stop milk from going sour by keeping it in the cow. Or Dad would look at the sports pages and tell us what a rubbish game football is and how the players are all overpaid crybabies and that THE ONLY GAME IS RUGBY, which is a man's game and not for namby-pambys. We argue with him about rugby being THE ONLY GAME, because Wills and I like football, except that we agree with Dad about footballers hugging and kissing each other and pretending to be hurt when they're not. And we agree with him that they get too much money, though we wouldn't mind if we were footballers ourselves.

So we sat there, Mum, Wills and me, all quiet and just eating. Then Mum told us not to worry about things, and that Dad loved us very much, and that we would go and stay with him as soon as he was settled. Wills pulled a face and said that he didn't want to go and stay with him and that Mum couldn't make him. Mum said Dad would be very sad if Wills didn't go, but Wills said he didn't care. I told him to shut up and that he was making it worse for everyone.

He stood up then and shouted, 'You shut up, Mr Goody-goody,' and stormed out of the house.

Mum and I washed up, with me thinking the house would soon be empty if everyone kept walking out, and Mum saying that Wills would be all right once he'd got used to the idea. I didn't even know if I'd be all right once I'd got used to the idea, but I was so angry with Wills for making everything worse, and I was upset too because I'd made things worse by shouting at him, even if he did deserve it.

'I wish Wills didn't always have to be so extreme,' I grumbled.

'I know, love,' said Mum, 'but Wills is Wills, and that's how he deals with things.'

'Never mind us,' I muttered.

'I know he has his moments, Chris, but his heart's in the right place and he doesn't mean any harm.'

Only when he's using me to entertain his friends, I thought.

When we'd finished, Mum asked if I would stay in the house while she went to the supermarket,

'In case Wills comes back,' she said. I offered to go out on my bike to look for him, but Mum wanted me to stay put.

I sat and watched the telly, even though there was nothing on. I sat there and missed my dad, because after breakfast on a Saturday we usually threw a ball around in the backyard, which was Dad's bit of exercise for the week, and we helped him to wash his car, which is his pride and joy. Wills never lasted very long throwing a ball or washing the car. He always wound up throwing the ball so hard that he bowled Dad over – STRIKE! – or he got carried away with the washing-up liquid, and Dad's pride and joy would disappear under a mountain of froth. Then it would just be me and Dad throwing the ball and washing the car, which was good for me, even when Wills yelled rude things at me from his bedroom window, and Dad threatened to wash his mouth out with the froth.

I sat there until the sport started, and Mum came home with the shopping and looked worried because Wills wasn't back. I said I'd go and look for him on my bike, because watching the sport without Dad wasn't the same. This time Mum didn't argue.

I cycled everywhere. Up and down the roads near our house, down to the canal and along the side of it, up through the high street and back again. I might easily have missed him there because it was so crammed with people who were wandering up and down, in and out of shops, as though nothing unusual or sad or threatening was happening to them, which perhaps it wasn't but it was to me. It made it more difficult to bear that life was going on as normal when there was nothing normal about it.

I spotted some of Wills's horrible friends. He wasn't with them and I wasn't going to ask if they knew where he was. I cycled past them quickly. I went into the library to ask Penny if she'd seen him go by, but I forgot that she didn't work there on a Saturday. So I cycled back home again.

'Wills?' Mum called when she heard me open the door. She looked a bit disappointed when she saw that it was me.

'I've searched everywhere, Mum, but I can't find him. He'll be all right though. He'll be back soon.'

Mum nodded. 'As long as he's not getting into any trouble,' she muttered.

We had lunch, then Mum did the ironing in the living room while I watched the rugby match on the telly. It was so quiet without Dad there. When Dad was there he would perch right on the edge of the settee whenever someone came close to scoring a try, and he would yell at the telly as though just by yelling he could make it happen. Wills would join in, leaping on and off the settee and getting in my way, so that if someone did score a try I would often miss it. At least I wouldn't miss anything today – except my dad, and even Wills a bit, if I was honest, because nothing was the same.

Wills still wasn't back by teatime, and I could see that Mum was beginning to get really, really worried. She kept looking out of the window and jumping at every sound that might have been the front door. I was so angry with my dad. He should have been there to help Mum; he should have been there to go and find Wills. But if he had been there, Wills wouldn't have disappeared in the first place, would he? So it was all his fault.

The door finally banged when we were washing the dishes and Wills's food was going hard in the oven. He came into the kitchen, sat down at the table and said, 'What's for tea, Mum?' as though nothing had happened.

'Where've you been, Wills?' Mum asked. 'I've been worried about you.'

'What's there to worry about, Mum?' laughed Wills.

'I didn't know where you were, that's all,' frowned Mum, 'and I knew you were upset.'

'Nothing to be upset about,' Wills laughed again. 'I just went down the canal with some mates. Come on, Mum, I'm starving.'

'It's probably ruined by now,' Mum scolded.

'I didn't see you down the canal,' I said, while Mum fetched Wills's food from the oven.

'You weren't looking in the right place, then,' said Wills. 'Anyway, we went to the shops as well.'

I didn't bother to say that I'd been to the shops too. I just wished Mum would tell Wills off for disappearing like that and putting us to all the worry, but I supposed that she didn't want to upset him again, that she just wanted to keep the peace, what with Dad not being there to help and Wills being in a good mood.

A loud crack of knife-against-plate was followed by a piece of pork skimming across the kitchen and on to the floor. Wills cackled loudly.

'Did you see that, Chris? Did you see that, Mum? Is that what they mean by "pigs might fly"?'

'Don't play with your food, please, William,' said Mum.

'I wasn't playing,' retorted Wills. 'It just leapt off my plate when I cut it. It's because it's so hard. Watch this.'

'I'll cut it up for you,' Mum said quickly, grabbing hold of Wills's knife and fork.

'Are you going to feed me as well?' giggled Wills. 'Pretend it's a train going into a tunnel.'

He opened his mouth wide and flapped his

arms like a baby. I couldn't help laughing, he looked so funny. Mum stifled a smile and told me not to encourage him, while Wills made goo-goo ga-ga noises then blew up his face, pretended to fill his nappy, and farted loudly.

'William, that's enough!' cried Mum. 'Not at the table.'

'Goo-goo ga-ga,' chuckled Wills. 'Dadadada-dada, Dada gone. Goo-goo ga-ga.'

Mum's face changed and I could see she was getting tearful. Why couldn't Wills just leave it alone?

'Do you want to play on the computer with me?' I asked him. I didn't really want to because playing computer games with Wills does my head in, but at least it would take his mind off Dad and give Mum a break.

Wills leapt down from the table and ran into the front room.

'POW, POW, P-P P-OW! Let's shoot 'em up, kiddo!' he yelled.

'You all right, Mum?' I asked.

'I'm fine,' she said. 'You go off and play.'

Wills had bagged the best controller and had pulled an armchair right up in front of the screen. There wasn't room for another chair, so I had to perch on the arm of his. A race game was on hold – GROAN!

'Ready, kiddo,' said Wills. 'You're bike number four.'

He turned up the volume as high as it would go and began to make acceleration noises.

'Go, kiddo, go, go, go.'

I pushed the button for 'forwards' and the one for 'fast' and I shot away from the start ahead of Wills and the computer-generated bikes. Within seconds I'd done a high-speed wheelie somersault straight into a rock and the other bikes surged past me.

'Great crash, kiddo!' yelled Wills, and then he whooped for joy as he overtook one of the computer-generated bikes.

I righted my bike and pushed 'forwards' again, more slowly this time, but the bike lurched sideways and back across the road. Wills was bouncing up and down in the chair now, and every time his bottom left the seat my perch lurched sideways along with my bike.

'I'm gonna overtake again, watch this.' Wills was almost screaming by now. 'Watch this, watch this. Here we go. Yeh! I am the cham-pi-on.'

His bike tore across the line in first place. Wills leapt from the chair, catapulting me on to the floor, and threw his controller across the room.

'Had enough of that,' he said. ''S'boring playing a cripple like you.'

He fell on to the settee, picked up the remote control, switched on the television with the volume up loud, and began to flick from channel to channel, barely stopping long enough to see what was on.

Mum came to the door. 'Turn it down, Wills, please,' she said.

''S'not loud,' retorted Wills.

'It is loud, and we'll have next door complaining.'

'Nag, nag, nag,' said Wills, and he turned it up as loud as it would go.

'Stop it, Wills,' I yelled. 'You're not even watching anything.' I grabbed the remote control from him and turned off the television.

'Goody, goody, goody,' spat Wills. He stormed out of the room and up to his bedroom, where he turned his CD player on loud and stomped backwards and forwards across the floor. Then it went silent.

'Now what's he up to?' sighed Mum.

'Leave him, Mum,' I said.

Be here with me, Mum, I thought. *This is the worst day of my life. I need you here with me.*

CHAPTER FOUR

We went to Dad's for the first time three weeks later, but he turned up twice before then to take us out for pizzas. Both times Wills refused to go, even though he loves pizzas. Mum pleaded with him, but he wouldn't even say hello to Dad, just shut himself in his room. Dad fidgeted his feet on the doorstep, his forehead covered with globules of sweat, and waited for ten minutes the first time, while Mum and I called up to Wills. The second time he only waited five minutes, his goodwill quickly evaporating, his anger becoming volcanic.

'Let's go, Dad,' I said. 'He's the one missing out.'

But Mum was missing out too, on a bit of peace

and quiet, and Dad was missing out on being Wills's dad. I was just happy to have Dad to myself, because I missed him like hell. I could catch up on the football and the rugby and how he was managing without us and what his new place was like. And I could ask him if he was going to come back. I could ask him if it would make a difference if Wills took the drugs they had been told he should take to make him calmer, but which Mum didn't want him to take because then he wouldn't be like Wills. Dad said that it wasn't Wills's fault that he had left, because as a father he should be able to cope with his own children, and that anyway there were other things. I tried to say that no one could blame him for not coping with Wills, but deep down I felt that Dad had failed us, all of us.

When Dad arrived to take us to his new flat, I thought I would be going on my own again, and I was looking forward to having him to myself for the whole weekend. That was the good thing about Wills's refusal to have anything to do with Dad. Dad and I would be able to do all the

Saturday and Sunday stuff we did before, but without the constant threat of a hurricane-force wind.

But no sooner had Dad rung the bell, than Wills tore out of his bedroom, down the stairs and into the front seat of Dad's car. Mum, Dad and I stood on the doorstep and gawped.

'Miracles will never cease,' sighed Mum.

'Come on, then, Dad,' Wills called through the window.

'Take them when they come, Rosie,' grinned Dad. 'Put your feet up and have a good rest. You deserve it.'

'Get a move on, Dad. Let's see this new shit-hole of yours.' Wills began to thump on the dashboard.

'Good luck,' Mum grimaced. 'Try not to get too angry with him, Brian. It'll only make him worse.'

Dad pecked her awkwardly on the cheek. I wanted to throw my arms round both of them to stick them back together, but Dad pulled away quickly and headed for the car.

Mum hugged me goodbye.

'Will you be all right, Mum?' I asked, wanting suddenly to stay with her.

'I probably won't know what to do with myself,' she smiled. 'Off you go now, and look after your dad.'

Dad's flat was only about fifteen minutes' drive away. Wills spent the whole journey jigging up and down on his seat, drumming indecipherable tunes on the dashboard in competition with whatever was playing on the radio. I tried to ignore him, gazing out of the window at the warren of brand-new, all-the-same houses that confused the route from our house to where Dad was now living.

'I need a wee,' said Wills, jigging up and down even faster.

'Nearly there,' Dad grimaced. 'Try sitting still and it won't feel so bad.'

Wills sat still but started to groan loudly. I could see Dad was beginning to lose it, before we had even reached his new home, let alone spent a whole weekend there. Volcano-meets-hurricane moments in the car were bad news. We'd nearly crashed once when Dad was trying to swipe Wills with one hand while steering the car round a corner with the other; and he had stopped several times in the past and threatened to make Wills walk if he didn't shut up, which was a stupid threat because Wills knew he wouldn't carry it out. I tried to distract Dad by asking what rugby match was on the telly that afternoon, even though I had looked it up before we left home. Mum's home. Before we left Mum's home to go to Dad's home.

It was real what was happening, horribly real. I didn't want it to be real. The only person I had told at school was Jack, and that was because his parents had split up a long time ago and I wanted him to tell me what it was like. He said he'd got used to it, and that there were some good things about it, like getting more presents for Christmas and birthdays, and not having to listen to his parents screaming at each other. But Mum and Dad never screamed at each other. They got cross with each other sometimes, that's all, and it was usually because of something Wills had done that had put them in a bad mood. And I would rather have no presents at all if it meant Mum and Dad staying together.

Dad pulled up outside a brand-new building.

'Blimey,' said Wills, 'is this it?'

'This is it,' said Dad, 'at least, the bottom floor of it is it.'

'You mean we've got to share it?'

'It's divided into flats, Wills, and I've got the bottom flat.'

'Well, you definitely haven't got a flat bottom – has he, Chris?' Wills guffawed.

'You wait till you get to my age,' Dad said huffily. 'Come on, out you get, I thought you needed the loo.'

'Ah, but you were never tall, dark and handsome like me in the first place,' continued Wills.

We walked up the short path, which was gravelled on either side, and Dad typed in a number on a security box by the front door. At the sound of a buzzer we pushed our way into a dark hallway and Dad turned to the left.

'Here we are, number two,' he said, turning a key in the lock of a plain white door with an eyehole at head height.

'That's what I want to do, number two,' said Wills.

'Thanks for sharing that with us,' I muttered.

'First on the right,' said Dad as we went in. 'And don't forget to flush it.'

Wills disappeared through the door, slamming it behind him, while Dad led me along the hallway, past two more doors, into a tiny kitchen. He stood there awkwardly while I looked around. It was so clean and tidy, not like our clutter-infested kitchen at home.

'Drink or anything?' Dad asked.

'I'm all right, Dad.'

'It's a bit small,' he said. 'Only two bedrooms. I'm afraid you'll have to share with Wills.'

'But −'

'I'm sorry, Chris. I couldn't afford anything with three bedrooms.'

Great. Just great. Share a room with Wills for two nights? I would rather sleep under a railway bridge than in the same room as Wills. Wills doesn't sleep. Wills rumbles and snorts and scuffles and fidgets, and when he's not doing that he's bashing around his room looking for something to do. It's bad enough sleeping in the room opposite him, let alone in the same room. As if to underline the fact, the bathroom door slammed, and Wills reappeared, still zipping up his flies.

'That's better,' he said. 'There's nothing like a good dump.'

'You've been told not to use that expression,' Dad said, 'and you haven't flushed it.'

'What, the dump?'

'The toilet,' Dad snapped.

'Sorry, Dad.' Wills looked anything but, and made no move to go back. 'Bit small this place, isn't it? Which room's mine?'

'I'll show you round when you've flushed the toilet,' Dad shouted.

'All right, keep your hair on.' Wills sniggered and loped off up the hall.

'He's upset with you for going, Dad,' I said quietly.

'I know he's upset. I'm upset. We're all upset.'

Then you shouldn't have gone, I wanted to say, but I didn't. We would just have to put up with Wills at his worst until he calmed down a bit, if he ever did.

Two doors slammed and Wills reappeared.

'Where's the other bedroom?' he asked.

'We're sharing,' I said, 'and don't make a fuss because Dad can't afford three bedrooms.'

'I don't want to sleep with you, your feet smell.'

'Not as much as yours.'

'And you snore.'

'Not as much as you.'

'Dad will have to sleep with you and I'll sleep in the other bedroom,' said Wills.

'You'll sleep where you're told. Now, what do you want to do today?' Dad was exasperated and we'd been with him for less than half an hour.

'I want to eat,' said Wills. 'Where's the grub,

Dad?' He opened the fridge. 'What are we supposed to eat? There's nothing in here.'

'You've not long had breakfast, and I was planning to shop when I knew what you wanted to eat tonight.'

'Pizza,' said Wills, 'since I missed out the last two times.'

'That wasn't Dad's fault,' I couldn't help saying.

'It's all Dad's fault,' said Wills. 'And now we've got to stay in this dump with nothing to eat and nowhere to sleep.'

'Shut up, Wills, shut up, will you?' I wanted to hit him so hard just to stop him from making things worse all the time.

'Look, you two, let's try and make the most of things, shall we? It's no good having a go at each other. I wouldn't have left your mother if I hadn't felt it would be best for all of us.'

Poor Dad, trying to bring the volcano and the hurricane under control. 'Come on, we'll go and buy some food, then I'll take you bowling.'

'Bowling, yeh, let's go bowling. And pizzas

tonight, eh, Dad?' Wills patted Dad on the back as if they were the best of mates.

'Provided that's all right with Chris,' Dad replied, looking at me questioningly.

I really didn't care, as long as it meant that Wills was happy, at least for the time being anyway.

We trooped back out to the car – Wills stealing the front seat again – and drove down to the local supermarket. Wills piled the trolley high with crisps and biscuits and ice cream and chocolate bars and fizzy drinks – all the things Mum didn't like him to have because she thought it made his Acts Daft and Dumb worse – while Dad sneaked some of them back on to the shelves when he wasn't looking.

'You're only here for two days,' he said.

'I might stay longer,' Wills threatened. I watched Dad's face drop.

We took the food back to Dad's then headed for the bowling alley. We'd been several times before, and Wills was much better than Dad or me. My hands were too small for the adult balls, so I had to use the children's ones, which Wills always teased me about, and I didn't have the strength to give it much pace. More often than not, my ball didn't reach the skittles at all before it disappeared down one of the side gutters. Dad wasn't much better. His own skittle shape stopped him from bending down very far, and he too was more successful at finding the gutters, even though he hurled the ball with all his might, often looking as though he would wind up going with it.

Wills, with his long thin legs, looked like a wobbly giraffe, but with his big hands he could pick up the heaviest balls and most of the time he managed to hit the skittles.

'Bags I set it up,' he said, as we reached our lane.

He sat down at the computer and began to feed in our names, but within seconds he was up choosing his ball and nagging at me to hurry up and finish it off. He'd put his own name in at the top, and was already taking his go as I entered my name. With his very first bowl he'd scored a strike.

'Look at that!' he yelled, and did a mad dance across our lane and next door's. 'Strike first go!'

'Well done, Wills,' said Dad.

'You're so flukey,' I groaned.

''S'not flukey,' said Wills. 'That's pure skill, that is.'

My own first attempt bounced, then trickled slowly slowly, into the gutter. Wills did the same mad dance as if he'd scored another strike, then clapped his hands loudly.

'Well done, bruv. Great shooting.'

'It's all right for you,' I said. 'You're bigger and stronger than me.'

'Bigger, stronger and handsomer,' said Wills.

'And very modest with it,' snorted Dad. 'Now, watch the real expert at work.'

Dad picked up a ball, rocked backwards and forwards from his heels to his toes, then charged towards the skittles, belly wobbling, and stepped over the line before skewing the bowl across the alley and straight into the gutter.

'Foul, Dad, that was a foul!' yelled Wills. 'It wouldn't have counted if you had scored.'

'Bit out of practice, that's all,' puffed Dad.

Wills scored nine with his next ball, then missed the remaining skittle, but his score leapt ahead because of the strike. I managed to clip two skittles but missed the remaining eight completely with my second ball. And Dad scored three and four, which he said showed he was improving already and you wait till the second game.

We were nearly at the end of the first game, with Wills having twice as many points as Dad, and me trailing miserably behind, when two older boys, four lanes away, pointed at Wills and waved. Wills seemed not to notice them until I pointed them out, then he gave a brief wave back.

'Friends of yours?' asked Dad.

'Sort of,' replied Wills. 'Your turn, Dad. Come on, I'm getting bored.'

Wills kept glancing over to the two boys after that, I noticed, though he was trying not to let anyone see. He bowled his next two balls straight into the gutter, and began to grumble that he didn't want to have another game. Dad argued that he had already paid for two games and that he wasn't going to throw the money away. When the first game was over – Wills winning it despite three bad last goes that rivalled mine – Wills dug his heels in and said that he wasn't going to play, and that Dad and I would have to play for him. When Wills digs his heels in, it's difficult to budge him. Dad was furious and neither of us could really be bothered to put much effort into the new game. Dad had been deprived of the challenge of trying to beat Wills, and I was on my way to another humiliatingly low score. Wills sat watching, unusually quiet, then disappeared in the direction of the toilets. I saw that the two boys were no longer at their lane.

Wills reappeared a few minutes later, on his own, just as Dad was beginning to mutter that there was something wrong with that boy's bowels. He sat down next to me while Dad took his go, and he smelt strongly of cigarette smoke.

'You've been smoking,' I hissed at him.

'Haven't,' he hissed back. 'The toilets are all smoky, that's all.'

'You'd better not let Dad smell you,' I warned.

Dad would do his nut if he knew that Wills was smoking.

The two boys, one ginger, one dark, reappeared from the direction of the toilets and walked past the back of our lane. One of them flicked a cigarette butt at me and sniggered when I flinched. When Dad turned round, they said goodbye to him politely. I was cross when Dad smiled and said, 'Goodbye, boys,' back, while Wills ignored them, got up and took my turn.

We went home for lunch soon afterwards, Dad happy that he had at least won one game, Wills crowing that that was only because he hadn't played, and me wondering how many more secrets I was going to have to keep from Mum and Dad. After lunch we sat and watched the rugby, just as we would at home, except that Dad's living room was tiny, with only one chair and a small settee in it. Wills tried to take the chair but Dad turfed him out, so Wills and I shared the settee and I missed half the action. Home from home, except that when we got too loud, someone thumped on the floor upstairs, which wouldn't have happened at Mum's because our next-door neighbours would have been watching as well. Mum's . . .

'You'll have to keep the noise down here, lads,' Dad whispered. 'The walls and ceilings are a bit thin.'

I wanted to argue that it wasn't me making the noise, but I didn't, and within minutes Dad and Wills were yelling at the tops of their voices and the thumping on the floor upstairs started again. Didn't those people realise that you can't contain a hurricane and a volcano?

When it was all over, Wills sat on the arm of Dad's chair to listen to the football results, so I went and sat on the other arm because I didn't want to be left out. Wills toppled into Dad's lap, and I toppled on top of Wills, and we fell on to the floor, all three of us, in a heap of tickling and giggling and screaming and punching (but not hard). It felt SO GOOD to let go and be silly and not care. I didn't want it to stop, but at last Dad begged us to get off. He crawled out from underneath us, pink-faced, sweaty-headed and puffing, and flopped on to the settee. Wills didn't want it to stop either and tried to jump on Dad again, but Dad warned him and Wills obeyed.

We sat on the floor, trying to catch our breath.

'That's what lions do with their cubs,' I said. 'They play fight with them so that they'll know how to fight and kill when they're grown up. Lots of animals do it.'

'You've been teaching us to fight and kill, Dad,' said Wills.

'We're not animals,' said Dad. 'We don't need to kill to survive.'

'Only if we hate someone,' sniggered Wills.

Dad cuffed him lightly on the head.

'What about in war, Dad?' I asked. 'We kill people then – to survive.'

'War should only be a last resort, if everything else has failed,' said Dad.

'I'd like to be in the army,' said Wills. 'It'd be cool shooting at the enemy – POW, POW, POW, GOT YOU, YOU'RE DEAD.'

'Unless they shoot you first,' I said. 'Then you wouldn't like it.'

'I think you've been playing too many video games,' Dad said to Wills. 'War is never "cool", as you put it.'

'I want to play on a game now.' Wills jumped up. 'Where's the computer, Dad?'

Dad looked uncomfortable for a moment, then barked, 'No computer, I'm afraid. Can't afford another one.'

'But what are we supposed to do all the time we're here?' Wills was beginning to blow again.

'The same sort of thing as I used to do when I was your age,' Dad replied shortly. 'Your mum's given me some books, and I've bought some board games and jigsaws —'

'Boring, boring, boring.' Wills thumped the arm of the settee as he said it.

I thought Dad must have fallen off his trolley if he believed that Wills would read a book or settle down quietly to do a jigsaw, just because we were in his house.

'And tomorrow I thought I'd take you to play basketball at the leisure centre.'

That stopped Wills in his tracks, and me too, if

I'm honest. Dad had never done anything like that with us when he was living at home. Mum's home. He felt he was doing his bit by kicking a ball around in the garden at the weekend, and coming to watch me play in a match on the odd occasion when I was picked. Wills is never picked for any of the school teams because he's too excitable and unreliable, even though he's a far better sportsman than me, and would be amazingly good if only he could concentrate and make an effort and control himself. Dad says I'm a grafter and that's why I get picked, even if I'm not the most skilful. I feel sorry for Wills when it comes to sport, because he gets really frustrated with himself and wishes he didn't have Acts Daft and Dumb.

Anyway, he leapt round the room like an over-grown lamb when he heard what Dad said, which meant that he fell on top of us again because the room was so tiny. He made Dad promise that we would go, and Dad said he would only promise if Wills promised to behave himself that evening. Wills promised, scout's honour and all that. Dad and I both knew that it wasn't within his power to keep the promise, but it did reduce the hurricane to a gale-force wind and even, for a while, to a gentle bluster.

I didn't get much sleep that night. Everything was strange: the room, the bed, the thumps and creaks from the flat above, the random noises from outside. The random noises from inside, the worst of which was Wills snoring alongside me like a hippopotamus. At four o'clock, he woke up and fell across my bed on the way to the toilet, then came back to tell me, with great hoots of laughter, that the thumps and creaks from above were certainly caused by somebody at it, even though they had been going on for hours. He then went to raid the kitchen and came back with a packet of biscuits.

'Hungry, bruv?' he asked, hurling two jammy dodgers at me, both of them hitting my head. 'You're supposed to dodge them,' he sniggered.

'Funny ha ha,' I hissed. 'Go back to sleep.'

'Can't,' said Wills. 'What do you think of this place, then?'

'Bit small, but it's all right,' I yawned.

'Bit small!' he scoffed, blowing crumbs over my bed. 'This room's like a bloomin' matchbox.'

'Dad can't afford anything bigger.' I turned my back on him, hoping that he would get the message that I didn't want to talk.

'He should have stayed at home, then, shouldn't he?' Wills persisted. 'It's because of him we've got to sleep in a matchbox and listen to people at it all night long.'

'If you were asleep, it wouldn't matter. Anyway, Dad says that's the central heating we can hear.'

'I've never heard it called that before,' Wills sniggered again.

I turned back round. 'Look, Wills, Dad's doing what he thinks is best, even if we don't like it, and at least he's trying to make things righter or he wouldn't be taking us to basketball tomorrow.'

'Bet I'll be better than you,' bragged Wills.

He began to leap around the room and threw a jammy dodger into the lampshade. 'What a shot,' he cried. 'And another, and another.'

'What the hell's going on? It's the middle of the night.'

Dad was at the door, skittle belly hanging over his pyjama trousers, hair sticking out sideways, sounding angry but looking like a circus clown.

'Sorry, Dad,' said Wills. 'We couldn't sleep, could we Chris? We're all excited about the basketball.'

'There won't be any basketball if I hear another peep. God knows what the neighbours must be thinking.'

'They're too busy –' Wills began.

'Shut up,' I snapped at him. 'Just go to sleep.'

The hippopotamus came back soon afterwards, but at least it stayed under the covers.

CHAPTER FIVE

When we signed in for the basketball session the following morning, the man in charge, Mr Columbine – 'call me Clingon' – looked at Wills and said to Dad, 'Is this one under fourteen? The under-eighteens train at a different time.'

Dad confirmed that Wills was only thirteen. Clingon whistled and said, 'Well, we can certainly use him up front.'

He looked at me then, and I could see that he thought I would be useless. I nudged Dad and whispered, 'Can't I just watch?'

'Get on with you,' Dad whispered back. 'You'll be all right. The exercise will do you good.'

'I'm too small for basketball,' I argued. Everyone there was taller than me.

'You'll soon grow,' said Dad, as though a
growth spurt would hit me the minute I stepped
on the court.

'Names?' asked Clingon.

'Wills is the tall one, and Chris is the short one,'
said Dad, just to make me feel really good.

'First time at basketball?'

Wills and I both nodded.

'Let's see what you can do, then.'

Clingon called all the boys together and ran
through the basic rules for those of us who were
'rookies'. Then he made us do all sorts of practice
drills, like dribbling the ball and passing to each
other. I was hopeless at running and bouncing the
ball at the same time. My feet kept getting in the
way of the bounce, sending the ball across the court
into the paths of other dribblers, who didn't seem to
have a problem, until I spoilt things for them. Wills
leapt around, whooping wildly, getting in everyone's way, but with the ball bouncing straight back
up to his hand as though it were attached by a piece

of elastic. Clingon kept shouting at him to quieten down, but Wills was enjoying himself and didn't seem to notice the mayhem he was causing. Clingon went over and spoke to Dad. Dad must have explained about Wills's Acts Daft and Dumb, because Clingon called Wills over and talked to him for ages, before patting him on the back and telling everyone to gather round.

He picked two teams and told the rest – including me – to sit at the side until he changed us in. Dad gave me a thumbs-up from the other side of the court, but I didn't feel like thumbsing-him-up back because I wanted to go home: to his home or Mum's home, I didn't care which. I just didn't want the embarrassment of being the last one to be picked, especially since Wills was in one of the starting teams as a shooter.

'Is that your brother?' the boy sitting next to me asked suddenly. He was pointing to Wills, who was pulling gruesome faces at the boy who had the ball, and was trying to get past him.

'Yes,' I muttered.

'He's a bit of a psycho, isn't he?' the boy grimaced.

'He gets a bit excited, that's all,' I said.

'Blimey, I bet he's a pain to live with,' the boy continued, as Wills stuck out his foot and tripped up another of the players.

'Sometimes,' I nodded. 'Not all the time.'

'He'd better watch it. Clingon doesn't put up with any crap.'

Just as he said it, Clingon grabbed Wills by the elbow and pulled him off the court. 'Take over, TJ,' he shouted to the boy next to me. He hauled Wills right over to the far end of the hall. I could tell by the way he jabbed his fingers at Wills's face that Wills was in big trouble, and getting what-for. Dad sat on the edge of his seat, watching anxiously, and looking over to me every so often.

When he had finished, Clingon pushed Wills back on court and took another boy off. What-ever he had said worked. Wills was still awkward and sprawly legged, but he wasn't so psycho and he didn't deliberately try to push people over or yell like a lunatic.

I hoped Clingon had forgotten about me, but he suddenly shouted for me to take over in defence. I wanted to be a shooter even though I knew I was too small. Wills was a shooter for the other team and I wound up having to mark him, which wasn't fair because he could just reach over the top of me, which he did, patting me on the head at the same time.

'Great basket,' yelled Clingon as Wills got away from me yet again. 'Try blocking him off before he gets into a scoring position, Chris.'

I nodded but thought, *Easier said than done.* Wills was running rings round me, literally. The only time I managed to get the ball from him, I tripped over his great big feet and gave it away again. I felt like there was only me and Wills on the court, and that it was a battle between just the two of us. But at last Clingon took Wills off and moved me into a position where I had to feed the forwards. I did all right then, well, all right-ish, and Wills and Dad yelled encouragement from the side, but I was certain I wouldn't be picked for the team if there was a match, and I was certain Wills *would* be if he could behave himself.

On the way home – Mum's home – Wills didn't stop going on about the baskets he had scored and what an amazing game basketball was. He said he couldn't wait to play again and asked if we were going to stay at Dad's the following Sunday. Dad didn't know, so Wills begged him and begged him, but I didn't know where I wanted to be next Sunday because I was worried about Mum now and I was desperate to get back home.

Mum was already waving at us from the front door as we got out of the car. Wills beat me to her. He gave her a big hug and wouldn't let her go. Then he pulled away and told her that we would have to stay at Dad's the following weekend because of the basketball. I gave her a hug and said that I would stay with her if she didn't want me to go, but then I was worried about Dad's feelings. Dad said he would talk with Mum and that they would decide between them. He pecked her awkwardly on the cheek again, ruffled my hair and pushed Wills playfully in the chest. Then he walked quickly down the path, jumped into his car, and drove away.

CHAPTER SIX

We don't go to Dad's every weekend. Mum doesn't want us to because she misses us, and I don't think Dad wants us to because when we're not there he can be neat and tidy and quiet. Wills went berserk when Mum explained that we wouldn't be able to play basketball every week because it was too far to drive from our house, and that she wouldn't have time to take us what with all the washing and ironing and housework to catch up with now that Dad wasn't there to do his bit. Wills said he would go and live with Dad, then. Mum said that wasn't an option. Wills rampaged round the house, then wrapped himself round her and pleaded with her to ask Dad to take us.

'I'm good at basketball,' he wheedled, 'and Clingon thinks I can make the team if I behave myself, and I'm really going to try to behave myself. Really, really going to try.'

He meant it. I knew that. Sometimes Wills is as frustrated by his Acts Daft and Dumb as we are, and I feel sorry for him then. The trouble is that however much he starts out trying, it never lasts very long, and then the feeling sorry turns to feeling murderous.

It was Dad who gave in. He said he would take us to basketball every Sunday, and on Mum's Sundays he would pick us up first thing then bring us straight back home afterwards. That way she would be able to catch up on all the chores, so that she could spend proper time with us in the afternoon. You would think Dad had bought him the biggest ammonite in the world the way Wills danced round him, and hugged him and wouldn't let him go. I looked at Mum and Mum looked at me and I said, 'I'll stay and help you, Mum. I don't think I'll be any good at basketball.'

'That's all right, love,' she smiled. 'You go with your dad and Wills.'

That wasn't what she was supposed to say. I was about to argue when Wills started begging me to go, saying that he didn't want to go on his own because he didn't know anybody, and they might get at him if he mucked up, and that he would behave himself if I went. I knew Dad wouldn't want to stay with him. Nobody else's parents stayed, and Dad had only stayed the first time just in case.

'I promise I'll be good, Chris,' he said, going down on his knees. 'Promise, promise, promise. Chris cross my heart and hope to die, kick my head in if I tell a lie.'

'I will too,' I growled. 'Only joking, Mum.'

I wondered what I had let myself in for, and why I had let myself in for it. It's what happened. I always wound up doing things I didn't really want to do because of Wills. Like the not-telling-Mum things.

'If you don't behave, Wills, you know what will happen,' warned Dad. 'Mr Columbine won't stand for any nonsense and you'll be out at the first sign.'

'I know, Daddy-waddy, and I'm going to be as good as gold.'

He was, too, when we went the following weekend. As soon as he walked through the doors of the sports hall (not before!) he turned into Mr Obedient. When Clingon called him over, he went over. When Clingon told him to put on a coloured bib, he put it on. When Clingon told him to practise dribbling with the ball, he did it. Even his great gangly legs seemed to stay underneath his own body.

Dad couldn't believe his eyes.

'Why can't he be like that all the time?' He hovered on the sideline, unsure whether it was safe to leave or not.

'It won't last,' I muttered, trying to concentrate on my own dribbling and hating every minute of it.

'Well, I'll be off, then.'

He headed quickly for the door. He looked as though he had been shot in the back when Wills suddenly yelled out, 'Bye, Dad!', but he didn't turn round, just waggled his fingers over his shoulder and disappeared.

Then it was just me and Wills. Groan. I was so uptight in case Wills decided to make me look stupid in front of a whole new load of people, that I made myself look stupid. I was rubbish at everything Clingon asked us to do, and I was one of the useless ones he left on the bench when he put the others into two teams.

Wills was one of the best, and he knew it. His height gave him a big advantage and he rattled in basket after basket. Whenever he got too loud or aggressive, or tried to be too clever, Clingon slapped him down with a few sharp words or a dagger-like glare. The amazing thing was that Wills accepted the slapping. *Did Clingon realise that this wasn't the real Wills?* I wondered. This Wills even tried to encourage me when, in the last five minutes, I was given a chance to play. Clingon might have thought he had Wills sussed, but he didn't have me sussed at all. I didn't want him to give me a chance just because he felt he couldn't leave me out any longer.

I was so glad to see Dad when he arrived to take us home. Clingon told him again that Wills had great potential if he could just keep control of himself. As for me, he said that I needed to be more confident.

'Get stuck in there, young man, and you'll do fine. You're too damn scared of it at the moment.'

I had to blush then, didn't I, and I wished I was black because then it wouldn't show.

'See you next week, lads,' Clingon said, dismissing us.

'He's such a dude, isn't he, Dad?' said Wills as we left.

CHAPTER SEVEN

Wills wasn't as good as gold at home. He was more messy than ever now that Dad wasn't there to yell at him to clear up, and Mum didn't have the time or energy after a long day's work and all the cooking and washing and cleaning. When we got in from school before Mum had arrived home, Wills would raid the fridge, plonk himself down in front of the telly, volume LOUD, and start texting non-stop on his mobile. Some days he would suddenly jump to his feet, waggle his fingers at me, and disappear out of the front door, leaving cartons, crumbs and wrappers all over the settee for Mum or me to clear up. He hardly ever did his homework. We were supposed to get it done as soon as we got in and before we watched the telly, and Mum and Dad and the teachers had worked out all sorts of routines for Wills to follow to help him concentrate and make sure he kept up.

But Wills didn't always come home straight after school. He'd set off, on his own, in the opposite direction, and tell me to mind my own business if I asked where he was going. Sometimes he'd come back really late, leaving Mum to worry about his work not being done, his tea getting cold, where he was and what he was up to; and me to worry that he was up to no good with his horrible friends, and that sooner or later I'd be dragged into it too. I didn't tell Mum what I thought. I just tried to tell her that Wills was big enough and ugly enough to look after himself. And he *was* big enough and ugly enough, but whether he could look after himself was another matter. All I know is that it wasn't fair on Mum, and it made me angry all over again with Dad.

Mum's too soft on Wills. When he came in late one day and she had to throw his tea away, I wanted her to give him such ENORMOUS what-for that he would be shocked into doing what he was told. If she did it just once it might help. But Mum doesn't have a hard button and her angry button is more marshmallow than rock. Wills only has to give her a big soppy grin, pat her on the head and tell her she worries too much, then she thinks what he has done isn't so bad after all. She forgets about all the times the teachers ring her about his bad behaviour, and about the times she has to apologise for him when we are out, and about the times he makes her cry.

I think she's tougher on me than on Wills, because she expects me to be good. She tells her friends I'm her little superstar and she doesn't know what she'd do without me. Sometimes I think it's not fair. I don't see why Wills should get away with doing absolutely what he likes, which means that I have to behave or otherwise it would be too much for Mum to cope with. Sometimes I feel like rampaging round the house myself, especially when Wills has been in my room and turned it upside down. Sometimes I feel like shouting rude words and doing rude gestures and not caring what anyone thinks of me. Sometimes I want to yell at the top of my voice: 'I'M HERE TOO AND I'VE GOT FEELINGS, BIG FEELINGS, AND I'M FED UP WITH YOU RUINING MY LIFE.' But I don't. I carry on being Mum's little superstar because she doesn't know what she'd do without me, especially now Dad's gone as well.

Then one day I looked into a shop and there was Wills. I was thinking about knocking on the window to make him jump, when I saw him grab a handful of chocolate bars and stuff them in his coat pocket. He saw me see him. For a moment he just stood and stared at me. And I just stared at him. Then he charged out of the shop, followed by his ginger and dark-haired friends, who had been hidden by the shelves, and ran off down the road.

The shopkeeper came to the door. 'Did you get a good look at them?' he demanded. He didn't wait for an answer, thank goodness. 'Bloody kids,' he spat. 'I'll have them next time. Just keep out of my shop, do you hear me?' and he went back inside.

I ran away from there as fast as I could and didn't stop until I'd gone round a corner. I fell against a wall, struggling for breath. My stomach had gone all nervy like it did when I had to sit a test at school, and like it did when I went on a scary ride, except that I didn't mind the scary ride sort of nervy. The sort of nervy I had now didn't turn into rollercoaster screams of excitement. This sort of nervy turned into feeling sick and wanting the ground to swallow me up in one big, enormous gulp.

My brother was a thief.

Even as I thought it and tried to tell myself that taking chocolate bars wasn't that big a deal, I remembered the ammonite. He'd stolen that too, I was sure of it. My brother was a thief! What was I supposed to do now that I knew that? What would you do if you knew your brother was a thief?

A hand grabbed my shoulder. I swung round into the leering face of Wills's ginger-haired friend.

'Hello, little boy,' he said. 'Something wrong, is there?'

I shook my head.

'Are you sure?' said the boy. 'You look as if you've seen something you shouldn't have seen. You didn't see anything, did you?'

I heard a snigger from behind me and looked round to see Wills and his other friend poking their heads out from a doorway.

I shook my head. 'No, I haven't seen anything, now leave me alone, will you?'

I tried to pull away, but the boy's grip was too strong.

'As long as you're sure,' he said. 'I wouldn't want you to suffer.'

'I'm sure. Just let me go,' I growled.

He let go, cuffed me on the head like I was his best mate, and told me to take good care of myself. The sniggers from the doorway followed me as I ran away.

I kept running until I reached the library. I checked I wasn't being watched and dashed inside, where I grabbed a book from a shelf, sat down and buried my head in it. I tried to read the words to take my mind off what had happened, but they all blurred into one and I couldn't make any sense of them.

'No "hello" today, then?' Penny sat down next to me. 'That's heavy reading for an eleven-year-old, isn't it?' she grinned.

I looked at the cover of the book and read: THE SILENT WEAPON: POISONS AND ANTIDOTES IN THE MIDDLE AGES.

'And they say the school curriculum is getting easier,' Penny scoffed. 'Not judging by that book, or are you looking for something to use yourself?'

I managed to smile, but I didn't know if I wanted to talk about what had happened.

'Let me guess,' said Penny. 'Someone's upset you, so you're looking for a poison that you can put in their tea without their knowing.'

'I wish,' I said.

'I think you need something more up-to-date,' Penny laughed. 'Poisons have come a long way since the Middle Ages. Talking about poison, and since there's no one else around, how about a cup of library best tea?'

'I'd rather have the poison.' I grinned in spite of myself.

'That's better,' said Penny. 'I've never seen you looking so glum. Has that brother of yours been upsetting you again? I'll be after him on my broomstick if he's not careful.'

'Isn't it boring in here when nobody comes in? I mean, what's the point in being a librarian in a library nobody visits?' I was desperate to change the subject but I thought I might be being rude.

'You visit,' said Penny, 'and I have my other regulars.'

'Not many,' I continued.

'You're right.' Penny grimaced. 'I wish we could drag people in off the streets so that we could show them what they're missing. Stuck on shelves, books just gather dust. But when you open them up, the dust falls away and the most wonderful imaginary worlds are waiting there to be explored. Not that I need to tell you that.'

'I'd like to be a writer,' I said. I wondered

immediately where that thought had come from, because I hadn't had it before. And then I felt stupid for saying it, because the chances of someone like me becoming a writer were absolutely ZERO. I'd probably end up in an office like Dad and turn into a skittle.

'There's no reason why you shouldn't be,' Penny said. 'As long as you have plenty of imagination, an urge to share the world that's inside your head, and an ability to bring it all to life with words. It sounds easy put like that, doesn't it? It's not of course, and I can't do it, but that doesn't mean that you can't try.'

'My teacher says I've got a good imagination.'

'Well, there you are, then, that's a start.' Penny smiled. 'Who knows, one day I might be recommending your books to my readers. Talking of which, I've been keeping this new novel aside for you. It's being heralded as the book of the year. Tell me what you think.'

I thanked her and stood up to go.

'Talk to someone, Chris, if things are getting too much for you. Don't bottle it all up.'

'What, dob on my brother? He'd never let me hear the end of it.'

I almost blurted it all out to Penny there and then because she was being so nice to me and because I was dreading going home and seeing Wills. I was dreading seeing Mum too, because of all the guilty secrets that were piling up inside me. I didn't blurt anything out. If I had started I think I would have gone all blubbery, and I didn't want Penny to think I was a crybaby. And what could she do? Anyway, Wills was my brother, till death us do part, worst luck.

When I got home, Mum and Wills were sitting on the sofa and Wills was being all butter-wouldn't-melt lovey-dovey. Mum looked happy like she does when Wills isn't being a nightmare, so I tried not to be grumpy even though I felt as grumpy as a hungry giant. Wills stayed lovey-dovey all evening and we managed to watch a film on the telly without him leaping up and down every five minutes. It made me feel sick though, Wills being like that with Mum – and acting as if he was my best friend. He couldn't just pretend nothing had happened because I'd seen him and I knew, and no matter how much his friends threatened me it wouldn't stop me knowing.

I WANTED TO HIT HIM. I wanted to wipe that soppy grin off his face and make him pay for what he'd done, like he was making me pay.

I went up to bed early. Mum followed me.

'Is there anything wrong, Chris?' she said. 'You're very quiet tonight.'

'I'm a bit tired, that's all, Mum,' I mumbled.

'It's good to have Wills so calm,' she said brightly. 'It makes all the difference. I expect it's the calm before another storm, but it's been a nice evening.'

I nodded and said goodnight. But it wouldn't be a good night – Wills would come in, I was sure of it.

It was two o'clock when he woke me by plonking himself on my bed.

'Are you asleep, Chris?' I heard.

'I was until some great oaf landed on my bed,' I growled.

'It wasn't my fault,' he said. 'They made me do it. Said I was a great wuss if I didn't do it. Said they wouldn't be my friends if I didn't do it.'

'Who needs friends like that?' I said.

'Most people don't like me,' Wills muttered.

'I'd rather not have any friends than have friends who make me do things I don't want to,' I replied.

'You don't understand what it's like,' said Wills.

He was trying to make me feel sorry for him! He should feel sorry for me! But I did feel sort of sorry for him in a way, because most people kept away from him. They couldn't cope with his Acts Daft and Dumb. They were embarrassed by it. At least they didn't have to live with it though.

'Mum would die if she knew what you'd done,' I said.

'She doesn't have to know, and you're not going to tell her, are you?' He was half pleading and half threatening.

'What else have you stolen?' I asked, and immediately wished I hadn't

'Nothing,' Wills spat. 'What d'you take me for? Just because I did it once, doesn't make me a full-time crook.'

'Keep me out of it, that's all,' I hissed. 'And keep your horrible friends away from me.'

'I was going to give you a chocolate bar, but I won't now,' he hissed back. 'Serves you right.'

'For Chrissakes, leave me alone, will you.'

Wills sloped away, but seconds later he was back at the door saying, 'Please don't say anything to Mum, Chrissy Chrissy. I promise I won't do it again.'

'You're always promising,' I growled.

'I mean it this time,' he said, as though he meant it.

'I won't tell Mum, but only because I don't want her to be upset, that's all. Now go back to bed and let me sleep.'

I turned my back on him to put an end to the conversation. It was doing my head in. *He* was doing my head in. Let alone my stomach, which was all nervy again. He would do it again. I knew he would. His horrible friends would make sure of that. Wills wouldn't be able to say no, and they probably thought it was a great big joke to get him to do bad things. I wondered if I should tell Dad. But telling Dad would make it worse and Mum would still find out. I was scared for Wills too, because I didn't want him to have the sort of what-for he would get if Dad knew. It would be like one of those big fights on the films where everyone shoots at each other and everyone dies.

I was so tired I didn't want to get up for school the next morning, and I could hear Mum having her usual battle to get Wills out of bed. I dragged myself to my feet.

'Why don't you just leave him there, Mum?' I called. 'He'll be the one to get into trouble, and serves him right.'

'Unfortunately, if he doesn't go to school he won't be the only one to get into trouble, I will as well.'

Wills was snorting underneath the duvet. He thought he was being funny, but Mum didn't and neither did I. I ran in and pulled the covers off him.

'Get up, you freak!' I yelled. 'Give Mum a break for a change.'

'You're so scary!' he mocked. 'Save me from him, Mummy, save me!'

I launched myself at him, but he wriggled from underneath me and tore off along the landing into the bathroom.

'Beat you to it!' he shouted and slammed the door.

'I hate you!' I screamed after him.

I stopped when I saw Mum's face.

'Don't, Chris,' she said.

She fled downstairs, leaving behind the look on her face to scold me over and over. I sank down on to the top stair and thought about hurling myself to the bottom.

At school that day, Jack wanted to know what was wrong with me.

'What do you think's wrong?' I snapped.

'I've never known you this grumpy before,' he said. 'Even Homer Simpson doesn't get this grumpy.'

'Homer Simpson doesn't have to live with Wills. If he did, he would be even grumpier.'

'What's Wills done that's so bad this time, apart from being alive?'

'Everything he does is so bad, and then I get into trouble for it,' I said.

'If I had a brother like Wills, I'd either kill him or kill myself,' Jack threw at me, before launching himself across the playground to join in with a game of football.

CHAPTER EIGHT

We got into a sort of routine with the going to Dad's. Every other Saturday he picked us up at ten o'clock and we went straight to the supermarket to stock up with ready-made meals. However much Dad protested, Wills didn't give him much choice over what else went into the trolley.

'We're from a broken home,' Wills said. 'We need treats to help us get over our broken hearts.'

'What a load of codswallop,' snorted Dad. 'Whoever heard of crisps and ice creams mending a broken heart?'

'Without them,' said Wills, 'I might fall to the floor, and all people will see is a blubbering heap of misery.'

That did it for Dad because he knew that's exactly what Wills would do, right in the middle of the supermarket, and it would be just as embarrassing as the pickled onions. So Dad gave in, and Wills wound up with all the junk food that Mum said he shouldn't have because it made his Acts Daft and Dumb worse.

It's always so neat and tidy at Dad's you wouldn't think anybody lived there. It can't be that he tidies up especially for us – NO WAY JOSE! – so it must be how he likes to live when he's not being our dad, which means it must be hard for him when he's being our dad and having to live with mess. Maybe that's why he left home – Mum's home. His new place doesn't stay tidy for long when we're there. I think he must dread us coming because of the mess, and the noise, and the thumping on the ceiling.

I dread going there. Wills knows exactly which buttons to push to wind Dad up, and Dad's fuse grows shorter and shorter. There's no Mum to help keep the peace, so I'm on my own, trying to think of things we can do that will occupy Wills and keep him out of Dad's hair – what's left of it. Dad gave in to Wills during our second visit and bought a games console – GREAT! – race games in a pea pod, just what I always wanted. The other thing Wills has decided he likes is Monopoly and he wants to play it all the time, except that he only likes it if he's winning. As soon as anybody buys a property that he wants, or charges him rent for landing on their property, or if he is sent directly to jail – DO NOT PASS GO, DO NOT COL-LECT £200 – he throws his money round the room and doesn't want to play any more.

There's nowhere to kick a ball around like we did with Dad at home, so Dad takes us to the park if the weather's all right. Those are the best times. As long as Dad threatens Wills beforehand that there will be no basketball the next day unless he behaves, it's good fun, apart from when Wills chops my legs from underneath me, which he does too often. I wonder for how long the no-basketball threat will work, because Dad uses it all the time.

'If you don't clear that mess up off the floor,

William, there'll be no basketball tomorrow.' Or, 'If you use language like that again, William, there'll be no basketball in the morning.' Or, 'If you don't do as I say now, William, I shall stop you going to basketball, and I mean it.'

I don't think Dad does mean it, because for an hour of the weekend he can leave us to Clingon while he goes home to read the Sunday papers, which is his favourite thing to do on a Sunday. I bet Wills knows Dad doesn't mean it, but so far he's not pushing it, which shows he can behave if he wants to. He sometimes sniggers though when he sees Dad is about to make his threat, and he leaps in first.

'I know, Daddy-waddy,' he says. 'If Wills isn't a good ickle boy, then Big Daddy won't let him go to basketball. Waahhh!'

When we watch the sport at Dad's, it's like being at home, except there's no Mum to bring us a cup of tea, and Dad tries not to yell at the telly because of the thumping on the ceiling. It's like being wrapped up in a cocoon in Dad's tiny living room. It's all nice and cosy, except when Wills bounces up and down on the sofa or drops food on the floor or swears at the telly, which upsets Dad. Then the last place I want to be is in that cocoon, but I think how good it would be if it was just me and Dad in there.

The night times are the worst. I bet you nobody could sleep in the same room as Wills. I've moved out on to the settee in the living room. At least there I can read myself to sleep without being interrupted every other word. It's a bit small and every time I turn over the duvet falls off, but anything's better than hippo snorts. I still get woken up though, when Wills goes for his midnight feast and comes in crunching crisps to watch the telly. He sits on me because he thinks it's funny, and showers my bed with soggy crisp crumbs. I try to ignore him and pretend to be asleep when he speaks to me. Eventually he gets bored and goes back to his bed. It takes me ages to get back to sleep then. I lie there, wondering how Mum is and if she's missing us, or if she would rather be on her own all the time because it's so peaceful.

The basketball doesn't get any better for me. I feel like a goat competing with a herd of giraffe. I keep hoping Wills will decide that he doesn't mind going on his own. NO SUCH LUCK.

'You're my guardian angel, bruv,' he says. 'It's like you're watching over me.'

He pats me on the head and I push him away. He's joking, but I know he's scared of being left on his own with nobody to stick up for him if he goes psycho.

'It's all right for you,' I moan. 'You're good at blooming basketball. I'm rubbish at it, and I feel like a girl next to all of you.'

'You look like a girl when you dribble,' snorts Wills, then he goes all soppy and says he doesn't mean it and that he'll practise with me and that he'll ask Mum to buy us a basketball ring to go in the garden. That makes me feel even worse, because he'll nag me to play with him twenty-four seven, as if an hour a week isn't bad enough.

'Why can't you get one of your friends to go with you?' I want to know.

Wills looks at me sharply. 'What friends?'

'The ones you're always hanging around with.'

'Not likely,' he grunts. 'Anyway, they're too old.'

That's the trouble. Wills doesn't have any friends his own age, not real friends, not friends who invite him to parties and sleepovers. Who would dare? Even my friends don't like coming to our house if Wills is there. They think he's hilarious sometimes, especially when he does things they wouldn't dare, but most of the time they think he's a pain the way he keeps barging in on us and ruining our games. It's much better for me if I go to their houses. I wish I could have a sleepover for my next birthday, but I know Wills would ruin it. He ruined my tenth birthday. Mum had invited a magician. Every time the magician tried to do a trick, Wills shouted out that he knew how the trick was done and jumped out of his seat to show us. One of the tricks was with a rabbit. Wills launched himself at the hat the magician was holding, and the rabbit escaped into the garden. We spent the next half an hour trying to catch it again, which wasn't easy because if you were a rabbit and five ten-year-olds and an elephant were trying to catch you, you'd hop it faster than a mad March hare.

You'd think the basketball would tire Wills out, but he's even more psycho when we get back to Dad's. He uses anything he can find as a ball, and shoots into the sink, saucepans and the wastebin. He went too far when he shot a muffin into the toilet pan. Dad said he'd been going to take us out for something to eat but now he wasn't, which wasn't fair on me, but Dad couldn't leave Wills on his own.

We went back to Mum's at four o'clock. Dad spent the hour before checking his watch, but even Wills was quiet on the way back. Mum came to the door looking pleased to see us and asked how we'd been, Wills charged into the house and demanded something to eat, Dad did the quick peck-on-the-cheek thing to Mum, and I wished he'd come in and sat down and told me it had all been a bad dream.

CHAPTER NINE

It's supposed to be better at home, that's what Dad said. That's why he went, so Mum wouldn't have to put up with Hurricane versus Volcano.

It's not better. It's worse. FAR WORSE. Mum can't handle Wills on her own, not now he's acting up because of Dad going. Even if Dad does lose his temper with him and shout and rage, Wills does sort of do what he's told – eventually. With Mum he only does what he's told when he's upset her so much that he's sorry. Then we get the soppy I-can't-help-it bit, which makes me mad because even if he is sorry, it won't stop him doing it again and again and again.

Mum hasn't got the no-basketball threat like Dad has. She says they can't both use it, and anyway she needs her Sunday mornings to catch up on things.

I go to the library all the time. Penny says I might as well move my bed in there, and I think how peaceful that would be. When there's nobody else around, she brings me biscuits and tea while I do my homework.

'No one else gets this sort of service,' she says.

'No one else deserves it,' I grin.

Jack came in once. He crept up behind me and put his hands over my eyes. I nearly had a heart attack because I thought it was Wills, and that my secret hiding place had gone for ever. As soon as Penny realised he was a friend, she gave him tea and biscuits as well. I told him he was jammy because she didn't do that for her other regulars, only me. Jack was so impressed that he came again, for the biscuits, not for the books or to do his homework. Jack's one of those annoying kids who always do well even though they don't seem to do any work.

'It's a bit of all right, isn't it,' he chuckled, 'being served tea and biscuits by some posh bint.'

'Don't call her that. Penny's my friend,' I growled.

'If she comes up with chocolate biscuits instead of these plain ones, she can be my friend as well. Shall I ask her?' He took a step in her direction.

'No!' I hissed. 'Just don't muck things up for me, will you? I have enough of that with Wills.'

'All right, keep your hair on. I was only joking. Anyway, how come Wills hasn't found out you come here?'

'Because he hasn't, and because he won't, unless someone tells him.'

'I won't grass you up,' said Jack, 'especially if you ask that Penny for chocolate biscuits.'

I kicked him under the table. 'Go away, pest, and let me get on with my homework.

'See you down the scrapyard later, then? Some of us are going to kick a ball around.'

'Maybe,' I said, and wondered if Mum would mind. Since Dad had left, I'd hardly been down there because I felt I should be home to help her.

He stood up and waved to Penny, who gave him a big smile and waved back. 'Don't forget the chocolate biscuits,' he grinned at me, and scooted off as I aimed a second kick and smacked my shin against the table leg.

I did go to the scrapyard. The scrap bit isn't there any more. There's just this enormous concrete area where lorries used to come and dump piles of metal rubbish, until people complained that it was an eyesore and they didn't want the noise all day and all night. It's still an eyesore, because the scrap merchant's building is falling down, and you can't go in there because it's dangerous, but the yard is great for football and skateboarding, and there's nowhere else to go.

Jack and six other boys were already playing when I arrived. Ollie and Sam are in my class at school, but I hadn't seen the others before. Jack called me on to his team with Ollie and Sam, and I was glad because I didn't want to be with the boys I didn't know.

'You dragged yourself away from your tea and

biscuits, then,' he smirked as I jogged in to join them. 'You're turning into a little old wrinklie.'

'I didn't see you turning them down, hypocrite,' I hit back with.

'The best place for a wrinklie is in goal,' he snickered.

I ignored him and ran into a central position. Almost straight away I intercepted a pass from Ollie that was intended for Jack, and began to run with the ball.

'Pass it on to me,' Jack yelled.

I ignored him again. I was enjoying myself. I was enjoying the freedom of running and not caring.

'Pass it!' yelled Jack again.

I didn't. I dodged round two of the players on the other team, and headed for goal. There was only one of their players left to beat now. He stood in between the two goalpost jumpers, fidgeting from side to side, betting I couldn't get the ball past him.

I lined myself up and took the most almighty swipe at the ball – POW! Everything seemed to go into slow motion then, like it does on the telly when they do a replay to show exactly what happened. The ball flew towards the net, I held my breath, the goalie dived, the goalie missed, the ball went through his arms and past the goalpost jumpers, I leapt in the air and screamed 'GOAL!' I turned round and Jack ran towards me, yelling, 'GREAT GOAL, WRINKLIE!' Everyone else was looking in my direction, and in the background, behind all the arms and legs, I saw Wills. I'm sure it was Wills, Wills and his horrible friends, coming out of the scrap merchant's building, and slipping away.

DANGER! notices were all over the building. It was all boarded up to stop anyone from getting inside. Was I seeing things? Had they come from inside, or were they just passing by? Why couldn't there be an action replay?

'Wake up, wrinklie!' I heard Jack shout. 'Just because you scored a goal, doesn't mean you can go to sleep.'

Someone flew past me with the ball. I didn't know whether he was from my team or theirs. I stuck out a foot anyway, and Ollie crashed to the ground.

'What d'ya do that for?' he cried.

'Sorry,' I muttered. I pulled him up and watched as he inspected the graze on his elbow.

'Nice one,' said Jack. 'You're supposed to tackle the opposition, not your own team.'

'Sorry,' I said again.

I tried to forget about Wills and what he might have been up to. I tried to make myself believe that it wasn't my problem. But the notices said DANGER!, and Wills was my brother – a danger to himself, Mum sometimes said.

It was like all the freedom of running and not caring had been punched out of me.

'I've got to go home now,' I called to Jack next time the ball went off for a goal kick.

'You're such a pain,' he said. 'We'll be one short again.'

'I promised Mum,' I said feebly.

'You're no fun sometimes,' he threw at me. I felt the sting of it because I knew he was right.

I took as long as I could walking home. It was late

afternoon and the shops were just closing. Everyone rushed past on their way to start their weekend, nudging, shoving, elbowing me as they went. I wanted to shout 'I'm here too!' because when you're only eleven and five feet nothing, nobody seems to notice you, and if they do notice you they still shove past as though you don't count.

I wasn't in a hurry to start my weekend. It was a Dad weekend, which meant it was a no-escape-from-Wills weekend. I wanted to see Dad because I missed him all the time, but with Wills there as well, in the cramped little rooms, it did my head in even more than being at home. I wondered if I could go to Dad's on alternate weekends from Wills, but how could I ask to do that?

I was just turning the corner at the end of our street when I heard feet pounding up behind me.

'Wait for me, bruv.'

Wills caught up with me. He threw his arm round my shoulder and bent over double, coughing and heaving as if he had just run a marathon.

'Cor blimey,' he spluttered. 'I think I might be sick.'

'Serves you right for smoking,' I said, smelling it on his clothes and walking on.

'Where've you been?' he asked.

'Scrapyard,' I said. I watched for his reaction.

'Scrapyard? Doing what?'

'Playing football. I saw you there.' I watched again.

'Me?' he snorted. 'Nah, you're imagining things. I haven't been near that dump.'

'I saw you come out of that derelict building,' I persisted. 'I know it was you, I recognised your clothes.'

'I'm not the only one with these clothes. Anyway, that building's dangerous. Why would I go in there?'

'Why would you do half the stupid things you do?'

He grabbed my elbow. 'Don't you dare tell Mum I was in there, cos I'll tell her you're a big fat liar.'

'If you want to kill yourself, it's up to you. It would do us all a big favour.'

I pulled my elbow out of his grasp and started

to stride away from him. He ran to catch me up. As he tried to take hold of me again, something clattered to the ground.

It was a knife.

Wills snatched it up and put it in his pocket.

'Where did you get that from?' I hissed.

'Found it,' he said.

'Where?'

'Just somewhere.'

'What are you going to do with it?'

'I'm going to throw it away so that nobody can get hurt with it.'

He marched up the road, turned on to our front path, opened the wheelie bin and threw the knife into it. He let the lid fall with an enormous clatter and snarled at me. 'Satisfied?'

I followed him as he stomped into the house and through to the kitchen, where Mum was getting tea ready. Wills didn't even say hello to her, just opened a cupboard, grabbed a packet of biscuits, disappeared up to his bedroom, slamming the door behind him, music on LOUD.

'Hi, Mum,' I said.

'What's wrong with Wills?' she asked.

'Everything, as usual,' I growled. 'Mum, can I stay with you this weekend? I don't want to go to Dad's.'

'Why ever not?' Mum stopped what she was doing and stared at me.

'It's so small there, Mum. It's like we're all on top of each other,' I said. *It's like Wills is on top of me, crushing the life out of me*, I thought.

'But your father will be really upset if you don't go,' said Mum.

'It's only one weekend,' I argued.

'If you don't go, then Wills won't be able to go,' Mum sighed. 'Your father can't cope with him on his own. He relies on you to help keep the peace.'

It felt like something exploded in my head then.

'I'm fed up with being relied on,' I shouted. 'I don't want to be relied on. I want to be able to have fun and do normal boy things and get into trouble sometimes and not worry that I'm just making everything worse. Like I am now, because now I'm being a problem just as much as Wills.'

I stormed out of the kitchen and ran up to my

room, slamming the door just like Wills. Then I began to cry like a big baby and that made me feel worse still. I heard Wills's door open. I leaned against my own door in case he tried to come in, but he went downstairs and I guessed that he had gone down to find out what all the shouting was about.

How dare I start a hurricane!

Mum knocked on the door and asked to come in. She opened it and stood in the doorway. Wills came up behind her and waved to me over her shoulder.

'You all right, bruv?' he asked. 'Do you want to play Monopoly with me?'

He wasn't being funny or anything, I knew that. He really thought he could cheer me up. He *wanted* to cheer me up. He had no idea he was the cause of my misery.

'I said stay downstairs, Wills,' Mum told him. 'I want to speak to Chris on my own.'

Wills waggled his fingers at me and galloped off downstairs. Mum came in, shut the door, and sat next to me on the bed.

'You're right,' she said. 'It's not fair that we rely on you so much. I suppose because you're never any trouble we tend to forget that you're just a child and shouldn't be saddled with adult responsibilities.'

'Sometimes it all gets on top of me,' I sniffed.

'You mean Wills?' she said, stroking my hair and making me feel like I just wanted to curl up in a little ball and go to sleep. I nodded my head and leaned against her.

'Sometimes I feel that I don't count because Wills takes everyone's time and energy.'

Mum held me tight. 'You do count,' she said, 'more than you could ever imagine, but it's not easy, I know, and I know you get a raw deal a lot of the time.'

'It's worse since Dad went.'

All I could think about then was that Wills was doing all these things that he shouldn't be doing. I wanted to tell Mum so that she could sort it out with Dad and I could forget all about it.

'Wills doesn't mean any harm,' said Mum. 'He just gets a bit carried away sometimes. He'll calm down more as he gets older.'

How much older? I wondered. *How much calmer? And how much more carried away was he going to get before he was older and calmer?*

'You don't know what it's like having him as a brother,' I said.

'Is there something you're not telling me about Wills?' she asked, turning my face towards hers. 'He's not bullying you or anything like that, is he?'

'Not exactly,' I muttered. 'Sometimes I don't like the way he makes fun of me in front of his friends,' I said rather patheticallly.

'I'm afraid that's something that all older brothers and sisters do.' Mum frowned. 'It's just a way of making themselves look clever, and Wills doesn't have many weapons in his armoury. Ignore it, Chris.'

He had a knife, Mum! It's in the wheelie bin. If only you could see for yourself.

'I'll go to Dad's, if you really want me to,' was all I said.

'It's got to be what you want as well,' said Mum. 'I'm not going to force you.'

I didn't know what I wanted any more, except

to stop the pounding in my head and the churning of my stomach.

'I'll go,' I said. 'I miss my dad.'

Mum hugged me tight and I felt her breathing stutter.

'It's the mess he can't stand, isn't it, Mum? His new place is all neat and tidy when we go there. It's like it isn't lived in at all.'

'He finds chaos and untidiness very difficult,' Mum agreed.

'So if we tried to be a bit tidier and if Wills gets calmer –'

I knew even as I said it that it wasn't going to happen, not just like that, not ever probably.

'I don't think he can be happy there, Mum,' I changed tack.

'He wasn't happy here, Chris,' sighed Mum.

A loud crash made us jump to our feet. Mum crossed to the door, turned and said, 'We'll try to protect you from the worst,' before running downstairs.

I followed her down to the kitchen where Wills was standing, eyes glued to the ground. The sugar bowl – or what used to be the sugar bowl – and its contents were sprayed all over the floor.

'I was making us all a nice cup of tea, Mum, and it slipped,' Wills moaned. 'I thought you'd like a nice cup of tea.'

'Accidents happen,' said Mum quietly. 'It was a kind thought.'

'I'll fetch the dustpan and brush,' said Wills. He walked straight over the sugar. 'It's all crunchy.' he grinned.

'I'll do it.' Mum tried to reach the dustpan and brush first, but Wills snatched them from her.

'I spilt it,' he said. 'I must clear it up.'

He started to sweep painstakingly carefully, but he couldn't keep it up. He began brushing the sugar past the pan, then brushing it back the other way and missing again. Sugar flew round the kitchen.

'Leave it,' ordered Mum.

''S'not finished,' said Wills.

'I said leave it!' Mum shouted. 'Just leave it and do as you're told for once.'

Wills dropped the brush and pan. He stood up

looking shocked. 'Blimey, Mum,' he said, 'there's no need to shout.'

'There is a need. There's every need!' she shouted again. She was shaking. I'd never seen her so angry. Wills just sort of drifted away into the living room without saying another word. Silenced.

Mum bent down and started brushing furiously.

'Can I do anything, Mum?' I murmured.

She shook her head.

'I'm sorry about earlier,' I said.

'It's not your fault.' Suddenly she sounded exhausted.

It was the quietest evening on record after that. We ate our tea without saying very much, except, 'Don't slurp your spaghetti' and 'Doh, I always splodge myself with tomato,' and 'You're the best cook in the world, Mum.' Mum left me and Wills to wash up the pans, while she went to buy some more milk. I was expecting the usual froth fight, but Wills just got on with the job. I began to think that Mum should shout at him more often, because it seemed to work, but I didn't like her shouting because she sounded like somebody else's mum.

We went to watch the telly when we'd finished. Mum came back and sat down on the settee. Wills tried to nuzzle up to her like a soppy dog, but Mum pulled away and told him to go back to his chair. I almost felt sorry for Wills because he looked as if he'd been punched in the face. He went upstairs to his room and stayed there, and I guessed he was doing his fossils. Mum didn't even say goodnight to him like she usually does with big hugs and big warnings about staying in bed. She just called, 'Sleep tight,' through the closed door. Wills didn't answer.

I heard Wills's door open in the middle of the night. The stairs creaked as he crept down them. I thought he was going into the kitchen on his usual midnight-snack hunt, but the noises were different. I was sure I heard the front door click open. I saw the security light go on through my curtains, but it did that quite often because of all the cats that prowled around outside. I got out of bed and peeped through the window. I couldn't see anything, but there was that clicking noise again, followed by the normal kitchen noises of cupboard doors banging and knives clattering. Wills making himself a sandwich.

Knives. Was the knife still in the wheelie bin? Was that what Wills had been doing?

Soon after that he came back upstairs and into his room. Did he have the knife with him? Where was he going to hide it? What was he going to do with it? I fell asleep with the questions buzzing round and round inside my head, like a fly that can't get out of a window because it's closed, but bashes against it endlessly.

CHAPTER TEN

Clingon announced the team that weekend. I wasn't in it, surprise, surprise. I was a reserve, but so was nearly everyone else who wasn't in the actual team. When Wills heard his name called, he went berserk. He galloped right round the outside of the court, whooping and shrieking and hollering like a baboon with a dart in its bottom. Clingon waited until he had come back, then grabbed him by the front of his shirt, pulled him forwards so that they were eyeball to eyeball, and growled, 'Any more nonsense like that, William Jennings, and your brother will play instead of you. Do I make myself clear?'

'Yes, Mr Columbine, sir,' said Wills. 'Thank you for choosing me for the team.'

'I hope I don't live to regret it.' Clingon let Wills go. 'You may be talented,' he said sharply, 'but you're also a pain in the butt.'

'Yes, sir,' said Wills. 'I know.'

Clingon stared hard at Wills as if he thought that Wills might have been taking the mickey out of him, but he wasn't sure.

Wills said quickly, 'I promise not to let you down, sir.'

Clingon went on to talk about the tournament he had entered us for, how his teams had always done well in the past, and how he had high hopes for us. The tournament was to take place in three weeks' time, and we would all have a chance to play, even the reserves. I was pleased and alarmed at the same time when he said that. I was sure the good players wouldn't want me coming on, even if I wasn't the worst one there, which I don't think I was. I knew Wills wouldn't want me coming on, and he said so when Clingon dismissed us for the day.

'I think it's daft letting the reserves have a go,' he aimed at me. 'If they're reserves it's because they're not good enough, and if they're not good enough and they play then we'll lose. Stands to reason.'

'You're not that much better,' I argued without much conviction. 'If the reserves have to be there, it's only fair they get a go.'

'Best they stay at home, then.'

'I don't want to play anyway,' I said. 'Especially not if you're playing. You never pass to me.'

'That's because you're rubbish,' said Wills triumphantly.

Dad arrived at that moment, thank goodness. Wills galloped over to him, threw his arms round him in a bear hug, and swung him round in a circle.

'Guess what, Daddy-waddy,' he cried. 'There's this big tournament coming up and I'm in the team and Chris is only reserve.'

He galloped away, picked up a basketball, ran the length of the court and dunked it effortlessly into the basket.

'Someone's excited,' grimaced Dad. 'Let's hope he can contain it. Well done, Chris. Reserve's good. When you grow a bit you could easily make the team.'

'I'll get to play,' I said. 'Clingon said so.'

'Even better.' Dad smiled. 'I'll have two super-stars to watch.'

'Are you going to watch, then?'

'Did you say you're going to watch me, Dad?' asked Wills, who had had the ball snatched from him by Clingon and been told to go home or else.

'Of course I'll watch,' said Dad. 'As long as you behave.'

'Of course I'll behave,' snorted Wills.

He didn't stop talking all the way back to Dad's – about how many baskets he was going to score, and how he was going to make Dad proud, and how he hoped Mum might come and watch as well and how he hoped Clingon wouldn't let me play for too long because it wouldn't be fair to me, because I wasn't quite up to it even though I had improved – (thanks for the compliment!). Dad told him off for saying I wasn't up to it, but I began to pray I would be ill on the day of the tournament so that I wouldn't have to play at all, because I would be bound to make a fool of myself and let Dad and Mum down as well as everyone else.

When we got back to the flat, Wills was like a kangaroo on a trampoline. He bounced from one room to the other, picking things up and lobbing them into the air, lobbing them at me, lobbing them at Dad. He bounced outside on to the courtyard and slammed and dunked our football, yelling, 'Great dunk, Wills!, 'What a shot!', 'You're dunking good, you are!, even though there was nothing to dunk it into except a wheelie bin. 'What a load of rubbish!' he shrieked as he dunked the ball in that. 'Not!'

At last, a window above crashed open and a red face shouted, 'For Chrissakes will you shut up before I dunk you in the effing canal.'

I thought Wills was going to throw the ball up in an attempt to dunk it through the man's window, but thank goodness he thought better of it and stuck his tongue out instead. Dad dragged him back inside and gave him a right royal rollicking, but nothing dampened Wills's spirits. By the end of the afternoon Dad was doing his nut. He loaded us into the car and drove us home at such a speed that even Wills shut up. We screeched to a halt outside our house. Wills tried to hug Dad goodbye, but Dad wasn't having any of it and told him to get out before he threw him out. He just nodded goodbye to me, which made me all resentful because I hadn't done anything wrong. Then he drove off again at high speed.

'Dad's in a bit of a mood, isn't he?' said Wills.

I couldn't be bothered to answer. I prepared myself to give Mum a quick hug then dash up to my bedroom before Wills started his kangaroo act with her.

Luckily, he seemed to have bounced himself out and, once he had bragged about being in the team, rubbished me, made sure that Mum would come and watch, he flopped in front of the telly. I went up to my room anyway after tea. I disappeared inside a book to the comforting sound of Muffin on his wheel. Mum came in to check that I was all right about being a reserve, and to ask if Wills had behaved himself. Then she asked if Dad was all right.

'Wills went a bit loopy about being in the team and Dad lost it with him,' I said, hoping I wasn't being disloyal to Dad.

'I wondered why he went off in such a rush,' Mum sighed.

'He couldn't wait to get rid of *us*,' I muttered. And it was true. He couldn't wait to get rid of us.

In the middle of the night, Wills came into my room and woke me and Muffin up.

'Go away,' I snapped. 'Can't you even give me some peace at night?'

'What if I cock up?' he whispered urgently.

'What do you mean?' I growled.

'The basketball,' he hissed. 'What if I cock up?'

I scratched my head, still not sure what he meant by 'cock up'.

'It's all right for you,' he said. 'Nobody's expecting anything from you, but they are from me.'

'Thanks.'

'But what if I play crap and we lose?' he persisted, and I realised how anxious he was.

'You know what Clingon says, that it's a team game and everybody's responsible,' I said.

'Yeh, but nobody else has, well you know what I mean, nobody else gets all sort of excited like I do, and I don't want to be crap and cock it all up in front of Mum and Dad. I want to make them proud of me, and then they might get back together and we can be a normal family again.'

Sometimes I wondered who was older, me or Wills. When Wills said all that, I wanted to tell him that a game of basketball wasn't going to make any difference. Even I knew things weren't going to change in an afternoon, even if we did win and Mum and Dad sat next to each other and cheered.

'If you just do what Clingon tells you, you'll be fine.' I tried to encourage him. 'You're the best player in the team.'

'Am I?' He looked at me with absolute amazement. 'You're not just saying that.'

'No, I mean it,' I assured him.

'You're not that bad either, bruv,' he grinned. 'Except at crossover dribbling. You're rubbish at that.'

'Can we go to sleep now?' I said.

'I don't know how you can sleep with the racket that Muffin makes,' he said.

CHAPTER ELEVEN

Wills missed school the next day. He went off on his bike as usual, racing ahead of me like a lunatic as usual, but I saw him stop and talk with his horrible friends, and then I saw them go off together in a different direction from school. I called after Wills. He turned for a moment but then carried on. One of his friends turned and made a rude gesture at me. It made me feel so pathetic and insignificant that I wanted to make the same gesture back, but I knew that would make me look even more pathetic, and anyway the three of them were too far away. Let Wills get on with it, then. Why should I care if he wanted to be a loser for the rest of his stupid life? I just hoped that none of the teachers at school would ask me where he was, because if they did I would say I didn't know and I didn't care.

Nobody did ask me, thank goodness. On the way home that afternoon, I stopped in at the library to do my homework. I didn't want to go straight home in case Wills was there and Mum wasn't back from work. Penny was busy with a customer when I walked in but she grinned and did a question mark thumbs-up at me. I did a thumbs-down because I felt in a thumbs-down sort of mood. When she did come over she was waving a poster.

'Cheer up, young man,' she smiled. 'Here's something for you to get your teeth into.'

'Posters don't agree with me,' I joked.

'Funny ha ha,' she said. 'Look, it's a national competition for story writing. Why don't you have a go?'

'What, you mean everyone in the country can enter?'

'Everyone under the age of fourteen. There'll be winners in two age groups – nine to eleven and twelve to fourteen.'

'I wouldn't stand a chance. And I wouldn't have a clue what to write about.'

I couldn't believe Penny was even suggesting it.

'You've as much chance as anyone else,' she persisted. 'You told me yourself that your teacher says you've got a good imagination, so finding something to write about shouldn't be a problem.'

'That's different,' I argued. 'That's just in our school. This is in the whole country.'

'Take the poster home with you and think about it,' Penny said, thrusting it at me. I'll help you if you decide to give it a go.'

I took it sort of grudgingly but I was intrigued as well, though I didn't let her see that.

'Anyway,' she said, 'why the long face when you came in?'

'Wills played truant today.'

'Ah, I might have guessed Wills would have something to do with it. It's not your problem though, is it?' Penny looked hard at me.

'I saw him going off with these two friends of his that are a lot older than him and not very nice.'

'It's still not your problem, Chris,' she said.

'That's for the school and your parents to sort out.'

I took a deep breath. 'He came home with a knife the other day.'

'A knife?'

'One of those fold-up ones. He said that he'd found it and he threw it in the wheelie bin when I was with him, but I think he might have taken it out again,' I explained.

'What would he want a knife for?' Penny asked.

'Probably just because when he finds things he likes to keep them,' I said, unconvinced.

'But you're worried that he's got it,' Penny said.

'A bit,' I answered. 'When Wills is with these friends he thinks it's big to do what they do.'

'Perhaps you ought to tell your parents, then?'

'How can I when I don't even know if Wills has still got the knife? If he has, I don't know where it is. I might be stirring things up when there's nothing to stir up. And I'm sure if he has got it it's just to go in his collection.'

I was trying so hard to believe it, because then I

could push it to the back of my mind and not have to worry about it again.

'Perhaps you could look in his room, just to put your mind at rest,' Penny suggested.

I nodded and wondered if that's what I should do. Then, if I found the knife I could throw it away.

'If you're really concerned though, Chris,' said Penny, 'then you must tell your parents.'

I nodded again, but I knew I didn't want to tell Mum because it would worry her too much, and I didn't want to tell Dad because he would do his nut, and there might not be anything for them to worry or do their nut over.

When I left, Penny came over and pointed to the poster sticking out of my rucksack.

'Forget about what Wills may or may not be up to if you can,' she said, 'and think about that story.'

'I'll try,' I replied.

It was really quiet when I got home, like there was nobody in. I found Mum in the kitchen turning the pages of a magazine. There was no sign of

Wills. Mum didn't say hello. She looked at me and asked, 'Did you know Wills didn't go into school today?'

I did the blush thing. 'He didn't go the right way, but I wasn't sure.'

'You should have rung me, Chris.'

'I wasn't sure,' I said again. 'Not until I didn't see him at lunchtime. And then I wasn't sure, because sometimes he doesn't have his lunch.'

'Why doesn't he have his lunch?' Mum fired.

'I don't know, do I? He just doesn't.'

'It's important that I know these things,' said Mum. 'If Wills doesn't eat properly it makes him worse.'

'I can't look out for him all the time, Mum,' I said angrily. 'I've got my own life to lead.'

'I know, I'm sorry,' she said quickly. 'I've been worried sick, but I shouldn't take it out on you.'

'Where is he now?' I hardly dared ask.

'He's in his room, refusing to come out because he says I don't trust him,' Mum sighed.

'What happened?'

'The school rang me at work and wanted to

know why Wills wasn't in. I rang him on his mobile to find out where he was, but it was switched off. Wills maintains that he came back here because he didn't feel well and that he's been here all day asleep.'

That's a good one, I thought to myself. 'He really expects you to believe that?' I said.

'I don't believe it,' snorted Mum, 'because I came home at lunchtime and he wasn't here. He said he'd gone out for some fresh air to make himself feel better. He must think I was born yesterday.'

'I did see him with two boys just before school,' I ventured, 'but I don't know if he stayed with them.'

'What boys?' Mum asked.

'These two morons he hangs around with. They're not very nice.'

I felt that I was landing Wills right in it, but what was I supposed to do? I couldn't keep covering up for him, and anyway Mum needed to know, if she didn't know already, that Wills was up to no good.

'Do they go to your school?'

'No. And they're older than Wills. They look about sixteen.'

Mum shot upstairs before I had a chance to stop her, which meant that I was most likely in for a roasting from Wills when he next got me on my own. I went up to my own room, closed the door and threw myself on the bed. I picked up the book I had been reading, but put it down again because I couldn't concentrate. Then I pulled the poster from my rucksack and studied it.

The National Tell-Us-A-Story Competition. First Prize in each age group: a dictionary, a thesaurus, 20 books of your choice and publication of your story in a national magazine. Second Prize: a dictionary, a thesaurus and 10 books of your choice. PLUS 20 runner-up prizes of a dictionary and a thesaurus.

Not exactly mind-boggling prizes, I thought to myself, even though I enjoy reading. I mean, money or a holiday would make you feel it was worth all the effort of writing 1,000 words, which was what they wanted. I liked the idea of having my story published, but I was never going to win first prize – NO WAY JOSE! Who was I kidding? I was never going to win any of the prizes, not in a million, zillion years. I didn't know why I was even bothering to read the stupid poster. I screwed it up and threw it across the room.

Mum poked her head round the door and said that tea was ready. Wills was still in his room, still maintaining that he wasn't well and saying that he wasn't going to eat, which proved that he wasn't well. He had told Mum that when I had seen him with his two friends, he was telling them that he wouldn't be able to meet up with them in town after school because he was feeling ill and was going home to bed. Mum didn't say she didn't believe him, but I know she didn't and I know she was worried. When I went to watch the telly, she took the telephone into the kitchen and I heard her talking. I think it was to Dad.

I went up to bed early to read, but I saw the screwed-up poster on the floor and the thought of entering the competition got into my head. *What would I write about if I did decide to enter?* I wondered. I didn't have the foggiest idea. At school you were given a subject and that's what you had to write about, whether it inspired you or not. But if you can write about anything – ANYTHING – how do you choose? I mean, there are so many things you could write about, how do you narrow it down to just one? How do you decide what the best subject is for you – one that won't be boring, or lead you up a dead end, or make you feel at every turn that all you're doing is writing about something that everybody in the whole wide world has already written about? Everything I thought about sounded boring, like MY BEST HOLIDAY, or MUFFIN THE MOUSE (that would have been all right except I couldn't think of anything much he could do – you can't write a whole story about a mouse doing wheelies!). I tried to think of something more imaginative. THE GIANT POSTMAN sounded more fun, but apart from scaring people and stealing their letters, I didn't know what else he could do. Anyway, I had this vague feeling that I had seen a book with that title in the library. That's the trouble. Everything's been done before.

And then I had a BRILLIANT idea. I would write about Wills! Or someone like Wills. Nobody could possibly have written about someone like Wills before. It would be about what it's like to live with a psycho. Nobody could possibly know what that's like unless they live with a psycho themselves. I could make it really funny because I could exaggerate the sort of things he does, like the pickled onion football – not that that needs any exaggerating.

Suddenly, I was excited about entering the competition. Even if I didn't win it would be good to write down how I felt about Wills.

I found some paper and a pencil and wrote the title: MY BROTHER. Just putting down those two words gave me a sense of achievement. MY BROTHER by Chris Jennings.

The bedroom door swung open and Wills's face appeared. I quickly sat on the piece of paper.

'What are you doing?' asked Wills.

'Writing,' I said.

'Writing what?'

'Mind your own business.'

'Snotty.'

'Snotty yourself. I thought you were supposed to be ill?'

'I was, but I'm feeling a bit better now. Thanks for dobbing on me to Mum. She didn't believe me because of you.' Wills sounded genuinely hurt.

'She didn't believe you anyway,' I hit back.

'She might have done if you hadn't stuck your big oar in,' he sulked.

'Mum's not stupid,' I said. 'You're stupid thinking you can bunk off school and get away with it.'

'School's boring,' said Wills, 'and the kids in my class are all donkeys.'

'It won't just be you who gets into trouble if you don't go. Mum and Dad will as well,' I snapped at him.

'It's all right for you, goody goody. You're not in a class where everyone's a year younger than you,' Wills snapped back. 'It makes me feel like I'm a right dolt.'

'Playing truant won't change that,' I said. 'You'll get even further behind.'

'Why don't you want me to see what you've been writing?'

The change of subject was so sudden I couldn't think what on earth Wills was talking about. Then I felt my face change colour.

Wills began to snigger. 'You're not writing love letters, are you? Go on, show us.'

'No, I'm not,' I protested hotly.

'What's so secret, then?' he grinned.

'Mind your own business,' I snapped again. 'You don't tell me what you get up to in your bedroom.'

'Nothing to tell,' said Wills innocently. 'It's just me and my fossils.'

'I wish you'd turn into a fossil,' I said lamely.

Mum called us down for a mug of hot chocolate. I had to watch Wills being butter-wouldn't-melt with her, like he is when he knows he's in the wrong and wants to be forgiven. Mum resisted for a while, but eventually Wills got round her and made her sit next to him on the settee to watch telly. I said I was tired and that I was going to bed early. Wills nudged Mum and said, 'I think Chris is writing lovey-dovey letters.'

Mum told him to stop talking nonsense, but Wills gave me a big wink as I went out of the door.

MY BROTHER by Chris Jennings.

I stared hard at the piece of paper, as if just by doing that I could make the words of my story appear. I chewed the end of my pencil and doodled all round the edges of the page. Then the opening came to me with a rush.

There's a hurricane smashing through our house. There's a hurricane smashing, trashing, bashing through our house. CRASH! BANG! WALLOP!

I read it over and over again. It was a great opening, I was convinced of it. CRASH! BANG! WALLOP!

CHAPTER TWELVE

Wills bought Mum an enormous box of chocolates the next day, and said that he was sorry for upsetting her, and that he would never ever miss school again, and that he was going to try really really hard to concentrate on his work so that she would be proud of him, and that he had spent all the pocket money he had saved up to buy her the biggest box of chocolates he could find to show her how sorry he was. Mum gave him a hug, but told him that he didn't need to spend all his money on chocolates for her, and that she would be just as happy if he knuckled down and stuck to the routines they had agreed on to help him with his work.

I made up my mind to search Wills's bedroom. I know it was a real spoilsport thing to do when he was promising to be good, but I had to know if he still had the knife, because I didn't want him to have it. If I found it I was going to throw it away. I was going to take it as far from our house as possible to get rid of it for ever, and if Wills screamed and shouted at me when he found out, then he would just have to scream and shout, because I wouldn't tell him what I had done with it. NO WAY JOSE.

I had to wait two more days for the house to be empty to grab my chance. Wills had gone off with his friends after school, and Mum wasn't due back from work for another hour. I legged it home as fast as I could, crashing through our gate just as our neighbour was coming out of her front door.

'You're in a hurry, aren't you?' she said. 'What mischief have you been up to, then?'

'Nothing, Mrs Hobbs,' I puffed. 'Just desperate for a —'

'Well, don't let me stop you,' she chuckled.

'– packet of crisps,' I finished, before dashing into the house.

I couldn't go straight upstairs. My heart was pounding so hard that I sat down on the bottom step and tried to calm myself. I felt like a robber. I felt as though this was someone else's house and I had broken in. I was terrified of being caught. *Why?* I asked myself. If Wills came home and found me, well so what? I would just give him what-for for being so stupid. And if Mum came home and found me in Wills's room, then I would tell her why I was there.

It was now or never. I tiptoed up the stairs and stopped outside his door with its ENTER-AND-YOU-DIE notice hanging from the handle. I tapped on the door, just in case, waited a few seconds, then opened it.

I'd seen through the door often enough to know what to expect inside. The room was like a landfill site, despite Mum's efforts to keep some sort of order. The only tidy bit was where Wills kept his fossils, on a bookshelf, all neatly laid out and labelled. There was the ammonite he'd shown me, in pride of place on the top shelf. I was surprised at how many he'd got. I picked up a shark's tooth, big and white and smooth, and imagined a whole row of them biting into someone's leg – CRUNCH! YEEOOOW! I could see why you would want to collect a shark's tooth, but I couldn't see why you would want to collect some of the other minerals and gems and fossils that Wills had. Some of them weren't even pretty, just boring bits of stone like you find in the garden or on the beach. Shells would be better, I thought.

I wondered where to start looking for the knife in all the mess that was strewn around. I stepped over several days' worth of used boxer shorts and socks, and smirked at the thought of Wills doing his usual yell of, 'Mu-um, I haven't got any boxers,' in the next day or so. I went to his chest of drawers and quickly opened one drawer after the other, picking up the clothes, checking underneath, then dropping them back again. Nothing. I poked around in the wardrobe. Nothing. I climbed on his chair and felt on top of the wardrobe. Dust. Years' worth. I crawled under the bed.

More stinky socks, a half-eaten, rock-hard cur-
rant bun, 92 million chocolate-bar wrappers, a
used dob of chewing gum stuck to the carpet, a
Playboy magazine, and a polystyrene carton con-
taining a few dried-up chips and a charred edge of
ketchup-spattered burger. Lovely.

I began to think that perhaps I was wrong, and
the annoying thing was that if I didn't find the
knife I still wouldn't know for sure that it wasn't
there. I was running out of time. Where else could
I look before I gave up? Where else might he have
hidden it so that Mum was unlikely to find it? And
then I remembered where they hid their loot in
gangster-type films I had seen, and police pro-
grammes where they advise little old ladies not to
keep their savings: UNDER THE MATTRESS. It
would be just like Wills to hide the knife there,
gangster-style (not little-old-lady-style!). I pulled
the bedding away from the side, plunged my arms
under the mattress as far as they would go and
moved them around. Nothing. I did the same
from the end of the bed. Nothing. No, something.
My right hand hit something papery. I grabbed

hold of it and dragged it out. It was a crumpled brown envelope, fat and sealed. I turned it over and over in my hands, felt its weight and the shape of what was inside.

It felt like money. Lots of it. What else could it have been, shaped like that (unless Wills had been collecting Monopoly money!)? What else would he have to hide under his mattress so that nobody would find it, he hoped? It couldn't just have been pocket money he had saved up. Anyway, he always spent his pocket money as soon as he got it.

The front door slammed. Wills. I bundled the envelope back under the mattress, straightened the bedcovers, dashed out of his room and into my own, threw myself on to the bed and picked up a book. I could hear Wills raiding the fridge. I tried to get my breathing under control. After a few moments there was a loud burp followed by Wills's great feet gallumphing up the stairs. I took a deep breath.

Through my half-open door I watched him go into his room, throw his schoolbag down, then bend to lift up his mattress. As he did, he must have sensed that he was being watched, because he dropped the mattress and turned. I snatched the book up in front of my face. Wills blew a raspberry and kicked his door shut.

He came out again soon afterwards and pushed my door wide open.

'You been in my room?' he asked.

My heart did an impression of a big bass drum.

'Not likely. I might catch something,' I muttered from behind my book. 'Why?'

'Someone's moved my shark's tooth,' he said accusingly.

'Probably Mum trying to clean,' I suggested.

'I told her not to touch my fossils,' Wills complained.

Mum's voice sailed up through the house. 'Hello, boys, I'm back,' she called. 'Anyone want a cup of tea?'

Wills charged downstairs and sounded off at her for touching his things. I could hear Mum calmly telling him that she hadn't been near his fossils and that he had probably moved his shark's tooth himself. Wills was adamant that he knew exactly where he had last put it and that it had definitely, definitely, DEFINITELY been moved by someone else, and that if she hadn't moved it then it must have been me and that I was a lying sod. Mum told him not to swear and that he was getting himself into a state about nothing.

'It's not nothing,' shouted Wills. 'It's not nothing when a little twerp goes into your room and messes with your things.'

I could tell from Mum's voice that she was struggling to stay calm. I decided to go and face the wrath of Wills.

'It wasn't Mum,' I said. 'It was me. I didn't mean any harm, I just wanted to see how many fossils you've got now, and I thought the shark's tooth was really cool.'

I thought Wills would go berserk at me. I'm sure he was going to, but then he said, 'That shark's tooth is 20 million years old. That's even older than Dad.'

'Cheeky,' said Mum, looking relieved.

'You can get even older ones,' Wills continued.

'The oldest shark fossil ever found is 409 million years old.'

'That's even older than Grandad,' I chuckled, hoping that if we could all have a laugh together Wills would forget to be cross.

'Nobody's older than Grandad,' hooted Wills. 'He's got more wrinkles than the world's wrinkliest tortoise.'

'Poor Grandad,' said Mum. 'That's from years spent working out of doors in the sun and the wind.'

'Dad won't get like that, then,' sniggered Wills. 'His skin should stay as smooth as a baby's bottom from being in an office all the time and from being fat, so the wrinkles all get stretched out.'

'He's not fat,' retorted Mum. 'He's nicely rounded.'

'You're only saying that cos you still fancy him and you want him to come back,' said Wills. 'But I won't let him come back because he shouldn't have gone in the first place, and that will be his punishment.'

'Shut up, Wills,' I jumped in.

'Don't you tell me to shut up,' he fired back. 'And don't you dare go in my room again or I'll break your scrawny neck.'

'Wills, stop it,' pleaded Mum.

'It's his own fault,' said Wills. 'He started it. He should say sorry for messing about with my things.'

'I'm sorry,' I groaned.

'So you should be,' said Wills. 'What's for tea, Mum? I'm starving.'

Mum closed her eyes briefly and took a deep breath. She opened the fridge.

'Fishcakes,' she said. 'Now out of the kitchen and go and do your homework.'

'Later,' said Wills. 'Come on, Chris, I'll beat you at that Grand Prix game.'

'Wills,' Mum said loudly. 'Homework, now. Remember your promise.'

'All right, Mumsy-Wumsy, no need to get snappy wappy.'

He went up to his room and came back down with his school books, which he spread all over the kitchen table. I disappeared up to my room. It wasn't long before I heard the television go on, and Mum's despairing voice urging Wills to come back and do his work.

I pulled my story out from under my bed and read what I had written so far. I was itching to write some more, but I didn't want Wills barging in again and making rude comments, and anyway I had homework to do as well. I was about to put it away when the next bit flashed into my mind. I grabbed a pencil and scribbled it down quickly.

A hurricane can cause total devastation. It can flatten everything in its path. Can you even begin to imagine that? Now imagine living with one. I bet you can't.

A loud shout from Wills made me stuff it back under the bed. I pulled my homework from my rucksack and tried to concentrate on fractions instead, but I started to think again about the envelope under Wills's bed. What was in it? Was it really money? Was he checking to see if it was still there when he caught me watching, or was he about to put something else there? And what about the knife? Was that there somewhere, and was there a link between the two? I wondered whether I dared go back and have another look.

When I told Jack about the envelope the next day, he said I should have opened it up the minute I found it.

'Cor blimey, Chris,' he exclaimed. 'Do you really think it was money?'

'It felt like it,' I said.

'How much money?' he wanted to know.

'How do I know? Fifty pounds. One hundred pounds. Two hundred pounds.'

'Two hundred pounds! As much as that!'

'Maybe. Maybe less, maybe more. I don't know what two hundred pounds feels like. And it might not have been money at all.'

'Why didn't you look?' Jack persisted. 'I would've done.'

'Because Wills came home, and anyway I wasn't sure I wanted to know,' I said.

'It would've been better than not knowing,' Jack argued. 'All you can do now is to keep going round and round in circles in your head, because you don't know.'

'And if I did know, especially if there was two hundred pounds, I would have had to go round and round in circles in my head, wondering what I should do about it.'

'I can't believe you had the nerve to sneak in there in the first place. I bet you keep thinking about it so much now that you'll have to go back and have another look.'

I did keep thinking about it, too, but I didn't go back to have another look. I guessed that eventually Wills would give himself away.

CHAPTER THIRTEEN

The day of the tournament was drawing closer. I was growing more and more apprehensive and Wills was becoming more and more erratic. Even Clingon was finding it difficult to keep him under control.

'Do you want to play in this tournament or not?' he asked him one Wednesday evening, when a practice match had been arranged, and when Wills had bowled over two of our own team in a wild attempt at stealing the ball for himself.

'Yes, Mr Columbine,' said Wills.

'Then play as one of the team and not like a boar let loose in a field of sows.'

Wills sniggered. 'Ugly looking sows.'

'I'm not joking,' growled Clingon. 'I won't allow the antics of one prima donna to ruin the chances of the team. Sit down and think about it. Chris, take over until your brother understands the word "discipline".'

That will be for ever, I thought.

I tried not to feel guilty about taking Wills's place. I didn't look at him because it would have put me off. Clingon kept encouraging me from the side, and I began to feel the exhilaration of competing instead of the inferiority of the weakest link.

I was getting better, I was definitely getting better, especially when I didn't have to play at the same time as Wills, like then. I could hear Wills trying to tell Clingon that he understood the word discipline now and that he was ready to go back on, but Clingon ignored him and stuck with me. I even set up the winning points with a dribble series followed by a blind pass, which one of our shooters picked up and threw for a superb field goal. Clingon congratulated me and the other boys slapped me on the back. I looked over at

Wills and read the pain on his face. It should have been his moment, not mine, but he knew he had blown it.

I went and sat down next to him. 'We'd have won by a mile if you had been playing,' I said.

'I don't care,' snorted Wills. 'If he doesn't want me in his stupid team, it's his loss.'

'Course he wants you,' I said.

'He'll have to beg, then, because I've got better things to do than watch a load of fairies farting around.'

'Like what?'

'Big-boy things, not little-boy things like basketball,' Wills said smugly.

Just then, Clingon marched over and took Wills aside. Dad arrived to take us home, and we waited while Clingon eyeballed Wills and poked his finger at his chest. We watched Wills nod his head several times, and Clingon finished by putting his arm round Wills's shoulder. Wills gave Clingon a friendly punch on the arm in return.

'I think Clingon's talked Wills round again,' I

said to Dad. 'He's amazing the way he can get Wills to do as he's told.'

'I wish I knew his secret,' Dad grunted.

'He's got basketball as a weapon,' I answered, 'and Wills respects him as a coach.'

'Lucky Clingon,' Dad grunted again. 'I wish he'd respect me as a dad.'

Wills bounded over. 'That bastard thinks he can say what he likes to me. He'll regret it when I don't turn up for his stupid tournament.'

For a second Dad looked flabbergasted, then he bellowed, 'You'll regret it when you don't turn up for his tournament because you'll have me to answer for. And don't think I don't mean it. I'm not having any thirteen-year-old son of mine making threats and using language fit for the gutter. Mr Columbine has worked hard for you, and I won't stand by and see you throw it all back in his face. Do you understand?'

'Why does everyone keep asking me if I understand?' shouted Wills. 'I'm not some thicko dicko. I understand, all right? I understand more than you think. I just don't want to be messed around that's all. Either they want me in the team or they don't, I don't give a toss, but I'm not going to sit on the dunce's bench just because I crop a couple of fairies.'

'Your attitude stinks,' Dad bellowed again. 'I wouldn't have you in any team of mine. NO WAY JOSE.'

'I wouldn't want to be in any team of yours, loser,' shouted Wills.

I thought Dad was going to punch him. They stood and glared at each other like they hated each other. I wished Dad would just leave it alone. I guessed that Wills's fears were eating away at him and that's why he was being so foul. The last thing he needed was Dad making him feel even more unwanted.

I realised too that a little bit of me would have been happy for Wills to cock up. If Wills cocked up then I would get to play myself. And I knew all of a sudden that I wanted to play. I wanted more of the congratulations and the slapping on the back. I wanted the spotlight on me. I enjoyed being the centre of attention.

My only chance though, of taking any reasonable part, was if Wills wasn't there. If someone else dropped out I might get to play, but I knew I wouldn't play well alongside Wills.

I hated myself for thinking it.

Clingon called for everyone to leave the hall because he was closing up. Wills loped out ahead of us. Dad wiped the sweat from his forehead.

I whispered to him, 'He's scared, Dad. Wills is scared he'll muck up.'

Dad looked astonished. 'Wills, scared?'

'He told me, Dad.'

'Why didn't he tell me?' Dad grumbled.

'It's not something you tell your dad, is it?' I replied.

'What's there to be scared about? It's not that important, is it?'

'It's important to Wills.'

Dad headed off after Wills and caught him by the arm. 'Hey, Wills,' he said. 'Let's not fight. Come on, I'll take both of you for a pizza before I take you home.'

'A pizza and a pudding?' Wills asked. 'We've

gotta build up our strength for the tournament, haven't we, Chris?'

I nodded half-heartedly.

'A pizza and a pudding it is,' grinned Dad.

'You probably shouldn't have the pudding though, Dad, should you?' cackled Wills.

'Cheeky monkey,' Dad growled. But things were all right again. Storm over. That particular storm, at least.

CHAPTER FOURTEEN

'How's the story coming on?' Penny asked me the next time I went into the library.

'Who says I'm writing one?' I replied.

'I know you are,' Penny laughed, 'because you say the same thing every time I ask you. Come on, tell me what you're writing about.'

'Three chocolate biscuits and I'll tell you,' I grinned.

'I'll expect it word-by-word for three chocolate biscuits,' Penny said.

'It's called "My Brother" and it's about what it would be like to live with someone who's a psycho,' I revealed.

'Ah,' Penny said. 'Taken from real life, eh?'

'Well, I'll probably add bits and change bits and exaggerate bits, but mostly I'm writing it from real life.'

'That's where a lot of the best stories start,' Penny nodded.

'It's got a great beginning,' I said. 'Well, I think it's good. I've talked about the psycho being like a hurricane, because that's just what Wills is like when he's doing his Acts Daft and Dumb.'

'Hurricane Wills,' Penny reflected. 'I like it. Go on, then, don't leave me on tenterhooks. How does it start?'

'I know that bit off by heart,' I smiled: '*There's a hurricane smashing through our house. There's a hurricane smashing, trashing, bashing through our house. CRASH! BANG! WALLOP! The doors are slamming, chairs are falling, cushions flying, feet running, voices shouting, 'STOP! STOP! STOP! STOP!'*

'That's a great beginning,' applauded Penny. 'It really makes you want to read on, which is what all the best stories do.'

'I've written about four pages so far, which isn't

that much because my writing's big,' I said. 'Wills thinks I'm writing love letters because I won't tell him what it is.'

'Poor Wills,' said Penny.

'It's not meant to be horrible about him, it's just sort of about what happens,' I said quickly.

'Well, if the rest of it is as good as the beginning, you stand a great chance of winning the prize.'

'No chance,' I scoffed. 'The thing is that I don't care about winning. The prizes are rubbish anyway. I'm just enjoying writing it. It's like I'm getting things off my chest. It's like a secret diary,' I said.

'I shall look forward to reading it when you've finished it,' said Penny.

'You owe me three biscuits,' I ordered.

'Three chocolate biscuits coming up, sir,' Penny saluted.

I went home as soon as I had finished my homework. Mum was in the kitchen cooking our tea. I gave her a quick hug, then dashed upstairs to change out of my uniform.

I opened my bedroom door. The draught from

it blew several tiny pieces of white paper up into the air. They settled round my feet. And then I saw. The whole room was covered in tiny pieces of white paper. Hundreds of them. I knew within seconds what it was. MY BROTHER by Chris Jennings. Wills must have found it. Wills must have found it and read it. Across my mirror, one word written in red flashed its angry letters at me. BASTARD! it said.

I went cold, as cold as if I had entered a frozen landscape and the pieces of white paper were flakes of snow. I closed the door and the snow rose and fell again. I sat on the bed and wanted to be sick. On a piece of paper by my foot I read the word 'jump'. On another by my hand I read 'cliff'. My feelings of guilt were overwhelming. Wills wasn't supposed to see what I had written. It was between me and those pages of white paper. He had torn the paper to shreds. What must he want to do to me?

Mum called us down for tea, but I couldn't eat. Wills was really quiet and wouldn't look at me. Mum tried to do teatime conversations like, 'Have you had a good day?' and 'How's the maths going?' and 'Only two more days till the tournament,' but she gave up when all she got back was a nod or a grunt.

'I don't know what's wrong with you two,' she said as she started to clear away, 'but I'd get more response from a pair of armchairs.'

'I wish I could turn Chris into an armchair,' spat Wills, 'then I could sit on him and crush him.'

'That's not very nice,' said Mum, looking surprised. 'What's Chris done to upset you?'

'I hate him, that's all,' said Wills.

'Don't talk like that, Wills,' Mum ordered.

'He's the one that's not nice,' Wills growled. 'Mr Goody-Goody, ha ha.'

'I'm not really hungry, Mum,' I said quickly. 'Can I go and do my homework?'

Mum shrugged her shoulders. 'Whatever's going on between you two, I wish you wouldn't bring it to the meal table.'

'It's nothing, Mum,' I muttered. I didn't want her to worry.

'It's not NOTHING!' Wills shouted, slamming

his fist down on the table. 'He thinks I'm a loony and he wishes I was dead.'

A shocked silence echoed round the room.

'I don't,' I protested. 'You've got it all wrong.'

'You've got it all wrong if you think I don't know what you're thinking,' Wills shouted again.

'I'm not thinking anything,' I shouted back. 'I just want to go and do my homework.'

'Stop it you two, stop it now!' cried Mum.

'Don't blame me,' said Wills. 'He started it.'

'Started what?' Mum demanded.

'Started writing nasty things about me, started wishing I was dead.'

'I don't,' I protested again. 'It's just a story.'

'Yeh, about me,' sneered Wills. 'Don't deny it.'

I couldn't deny it, but it wasn't meant to do any harm. Wills wasn't supposed to know anything about it.

'Makes me sound like a right git,' Wills spat.

'That's enough, Wills,' ordered Mum. 'What is it, this story, Chris?'

'Just something I was writing for a competition. Nothing important.'

'He just wants to tell the whole world a load of lies about me, that's all,' said Wills.

'I wasn't going to send it in anyway,' I said.

'Where is the story?' Mum asked.

I looked at Wills and he stared back at me. 'I've torn it up,' I said, holding his gaze.

'Best thing for it,' Wills pronounced.

'If he's torn it up, what's all the fuss about?' Mum looked genuinely puzzled.

'Doesn't mean he didn't write it in the first place,' Wills said. 'Doesn't mean he isn't still thinking it. Doesn't mean he doesn't want me to jump off a cliff.'

'I've had enough,' I almost shouted. 'I'm going to do my homework.'

I tore out of the kitchen and up into my bedroom as fast as I could, slamming the bedroom door behind me. Wills was doing my head in going round and round in cirlces like that. I scrubbed the accusing letters from my mirror, then began to pick up the numberless pieces of paper, screwing them into a ball as I went in the hope of destroying their ability to blame me.

Mum came in when I was halfway through. She sat on the bed and said that whatever I had written had really upset Wills.

'He's always upsetting me,' I retorted. 'Every minute of every day he upsets me. But that doesn't matter because I'm supposed to be able to cope. Anyway, Wills is exaggerating everything as usual.'

'Maybe it wasn't the best thing to write about,' Mum said quietly.

'It was the best thing for me,' I argued, 'and Wills wasn't supposed to see it.'

'Well, the damage is done now,' Mum sighed. 'Look, I'm not blaming you, Chris, it's just a pity Wills had to find it.'

'Then he should keep out of my room like I keep out of his,' I growled, and bit my tongue straightaway because I'd been digging up guilty secrets in Wills's room as well.

Mum sat for a moment lost in thought, before asking me gently, 'What was the competition anyway?'

'It doesn't matter any more,' I muttered.

Later on, I heard Wills go into his room. After a

few moments, I got up from my bed and knocked on his door.

'Wills,' I said.

No answer.

'Wills,' I tried again.

'Don't want to speak to you.'

I opened the door and hovered in the doorway. 'It's just a story. I didn't mean any harm by it. I'm sorry, all right?'

'It's about me and how horrible it is living with me,' he snarled.

'You shouldn't have gone into my room. You don't like it if I go into your room,' I said, trying to be patient.

'There's nothing to hide in my room,' he said smugly.

'Isn't there?' What about under your mattress?' I blurted out.

Wills went very silent. At last, without looking at me, he said, 'You've been watching too many little-boy films.'

'There's an envelope under your mattress and it's got money in it, lots of it,' I hissed.

'Is there?' said Wills. 'Blimey, I could do with some money.'

He jumped off the bed, lifted the mattress up as high as he could, and peered underneath.

'Like I said,' he grinned at me. 'You've been watching too many films.'

'There was an envelope there and you know it,' I said savagely.

I didn't wait for him to deny it. There was no point in arguing. The envelope had gone. No knife. No envelope. No story.

CHAPTER FIFTEEN

I started to get not-very-nice messages on my mobile after that. Mostly it was rude names and stupid stuff like that. Those were from Wills. But there were others, more threatening, which came from numbers I didn't recognise and which told me in graphic detail what would happen to me if I tried to get Wills into trouble. I know they were from Wills's friends, and that he must have given them my number, but I couldn't believe he knew what they were writing.

I wasn't really scared, but you wouldn't like it if your mobile told you you had a message and you kept finding it was something you didn't want to read, especially if you knew that the person who sent it was having a good laugh thinking about the effect it was having on you. I began to leave my mobile switched off, and sometimes I didn't even take it with me when I went out, because when one of those messages came it got me in a bad mood. That meant that I missed important messages, like when Jack wanted me to meet him at the scrapyard to help him practise ball skills, because he had a chance of being football captain. And when Mum asked me to pick up some chicken for tea because she had forgotten and didn't have time, so we ended up eating potatoes and broccoli and carrots with scrambled egg. And when Dad sent me a 'What did you think of the rugby last night?' message and went all huffy, because he thought I was off with him and hadn't bothered to reply, which I would have done because it was a GREAT match, and Dad supports the team that won.

When Wills was at home he acted as though nothing had happened, and as though we were all right with each other. I pretended nothing was happening as well, because I thought if I didn't react his friends would get bored and stop having a go at me. Mum said she was glad that we had made up. She wanted me to enter the story competition with a different story, but I didn't want to, NO WAY JOSE. I was too upset at seeing MY BROTHER ripped to shreds, and I was secretly determined that one day I would write that story again, for myself.

It was a Dad weekend the weekend following the story storm. On Saturday morning, Wills announced that he didn't want to go, that no one could make him go, that he had better things to do, and that if Dad wanted to see him then he should make the effort and come home. Mum tried to persuade him, but he dug his heels in, and when Dad arrived to pick us up he was still refusing to go. Dad didn't make a fuss, and he didn't try to change Wills's mind. I was pleased. I was looking forward to my first Wills-free time with Dad. Then Dad went and spoilt it by saying that he had bought a brand-new computer with a new game to play on it, and that he couldn't wait to take me on. Wills jumped up from the settee.

'Cor blimey, Dad,' he said. 'I'm the one you should be taking on if you want a challenge.'

'You said you'd got better things to do,' I protested.

'They can wait,' said Wills.

'It's nice to know that it's my company you can't do without,' grimaced Dad. 'I'd hate to think I was less of a draw than a computer game.'

'Don't you worry, Dad,' smirked Wills. 'The computer game is far more of a draw.'

'Does that mean you're coming, then?' asked Dad.

'It sure does, Daddy-O,' said Wills. 'I'll just get my stuff.'

I think Dad could tell from the look on my face that I was disappointed. 'Perhaps we could go out together one evening, just you and me,' he said.

I nodded, but I thought it was just one of those things that Dad says sometimes but forgets about. Wills came charging back down the stairs, pushed past me and bagged the front seat of the car, as usual.

'Come on, you two,' he yelled from the window, then he started sending text messages on his mobile, and I wondered if any of them were to me. Just as we reached Dad's, a message came through to him and when he read it he became very agitated. He sent another message back, then threw his mobile into the well of the car when the response came.

'Girlfriend?' chuckled Dad.

'Funny ha ha,' scowled Wills. 'I wish I hadn't come now.'

'I can always take you back,' said Dad.

I wish you would, I thought. I could see it was going to be a lousy weekend.

'You'd like that, wouldn't you?' Wills challenged Dad. 'And you,' he aimed at me.

'For goodness sake, Wills, stop twisting things,' said Dad. 'I thought we were all going to have a fun weekend together.'

'It's not fun being with you,' growled Wills. 'You treat me like I'm some sort of idiot.'

'What are you talking about, Wills?' Dad protested. 'What have I done?'

'You left home because of me, that's what

you've done,' Wills cried. 'And Mr Goody-goody here is always trying to get me into trouble.'

'Of course he's not,' argued Dad, 'and I didn't leave home because of you. I left home because of me. Because of me, Wills. Because I was making things worse. Because I'm not good at being a dad.'

'You are a good dad,' I jumped in with, stung by Wills's accusations.

'It's because of you I can't see my friends when I want to,' shouted Wills.

'If you want to see your friends, I'll take you to see your friends.' Dad's voice was getting louder too.

'It's too late now,' Wills said sulkily.

'I'm not forcing you to come and stay with me. I'd like you to stay with me, but if you'd rather be with your friends then I understand.'

'They won't want me now, because I said I was coming with you instead of seeing them, and they think I'm a girl because I didn't refuse.'

'Nice friends,' muttered Dad.

'At least they respect me,' Wills challenged.

'Sounds like it,' said Dad.

'What would you know?'

Dad wiped the sweat from his forehead. I felt sorry for him. He had been dragged into a confrontation he hadn't expected and didn't understand. I understood. I'd seen Wills's friends in action. I knew what they were like and I guessed that they would give Wills a hard time if he didn't do what they wanted. Not that Wills would ever believe that, because he wouldn't want to believe it.

Dad took a deep breath. 'Wills,' he began, 'can we start this weekend again? Let's order some pizzas and get on that computer so that you can thrash the pants off me, and then we'll watch the big match. What do you say, Chris?'

I saw Dad's look of desperation.

'Yeh, come on Wills, you can thrash the pants off me as well,' I said without much enthusiasm.

'Too easy,' grumbled Wills, but he got out of the car and loped up to the front door, pushed through it, and knocked loudly on the door of Dad's flat as though he was expecting someone to answer it.

'There's no one in,' said Dad.

'Typical,' scoffed Wills. 'I give up seeing my friends to come and stay with my dad, and he's not even here.'

'Just a minute,' said Dad.

He pushed past Wills, unlocked the door, went inside and closed it behind him.

'Now knock,' he yelled.

Wills knocked. Dad opened the door.

'Wills! Chris!' he exclaimed. 'How wonderful to see you! Come in, come in.'

'Wonderful to see you too, Daddy-waddy,' said Wills. 'What's to eat?'

'Shall we order some pizzas?' asked Dad.

'Yeh, pizzas,' said Wills.

'And garlic bread,' I added.

'And Coke,' said Wills.

'All right,' said Dad. 'Coke as well. I'll ring them now.'

I wished it could always be like that, the being friends and the being silly, instead of the shouting and the angry words. It used to be like that more often when Dad was at home, even if the Volcano versus the Hurricane was devastating when it happened. At least everyone seemed to be happier in-between. Now we all seemed to spend our days upsetting each other, even when we didn't mean to. I wished Dad could see that it was better before, and that Wills had got worse since he left. Or was it Wills's horrible friends who had made him worse?

That night, after Wills had thrashed me and Dad at the new computer game, and after we had gone mad watching the rugby, and after we had played pool at the pub round the corner, and when I was trying to go to sleep in the bedroom (Dad didn't want me sleeping on the settee) and Wills was tossing and turning like a bundle of sheets in a tumble dryer, Wills suddenly said:

'What would you do if you had to do something because you were sort of expected to do it, and you might get into trouble if you didn't do it, but you didn't really want to do it any more, and perhaps you never wanted to do it in the first place, but you got sort of persuaded?'

'What?' I replied. I hadn't got a clue what he was talking about.

'Well, say, for example, you were supposed to go somewhere to do something and you didn't want to go, but you would get into trouble if you didn't go, what would you do?'

'Depends what it was and what sort of trouble I would get into, I suppose,' I said.

I looked across the darkened room at him. I could just make out his shape. He was lying on his back in bed, one hand up behind his head, the other twisting a corner of his sheet into a knot.

'You're not talking about not wanting to come here, are you?' I asked, 'Because Dad's already said you don't have to if you don't want to.'

'Course not,' muttered Wills.

'Are you still worried about the tournament, then?' I tried.

'Who says I'm talking about me?' said Wills. 'Anyway, why wouldn't I want to play in the tournament?'

I was dumbfounded by how easily Wills

could forget things, or just push them out of his mind.

'I just thought you might be worrying about your – well, you know, like you said, about how you get a bit carried away sometimes and not wanting to let Mum and Dad down and all that,' I said nervously.

'You mean my "Acts Daft and Dumb", as you so nicely put it,' Wills hissed.

I shifted uncomfortably, but didn't answer.

'It doesn't matter,' said Wills. 'I expect the person I'm talking about will sort it out himself.'

He went quiet, but he began to motor round in his bed again, and I was wide awake lying there listening to him. I knew he was wide awake too because there were no hippo snorts.

'Wills,' I said.

'What now?' he replied.

'You know those friends of yours – the ginger one and the dark-haired one?'

There was a silence before he said, 'What about them?'

'Are they all right with you?' I ventured.

'What do you mean "all right with me"?'

'Well, they are nice to you, aren't they?'

'That's a stupid question, isn't it?' said Wills sharply. 'Course they're all right with me, they're my friends, aren't they?'

'They don't seem very friendly to me,' I said.

'Well, they're not your friends, are they?' Wills chortled. 'They look out for me though.'

'Aren't they a bit old for you?'

'You sound like Mum. That's the sort of thing she would say. Anyway, all the kids my age are namby-pamby babies – especially the ones at school – and they don't like me, because I'm not in the same year as them.'

'Don't your friends boss you around cos they're older?' I wanted to know.

'Nobody bosses Wills around,' said Wills, talking like he had just come out of an American film. 'Anyway, what do you care?'

I shrugged my shoulders. 'I don't really,' I said. 'I just wondered.'

'I do what I want to do, and if I don't want to

do it, I don't do it. Now shut up and go to sleep, will you.'

Wills turned away from me to terminate the conversation, and I was left to puzzle out what he had been on about in the first place.

CHAPTER SIXTEEN

I went to the library in the week. I wanted to talk to Penny about how I was feeling about playing in the tournament. The final practice had been brilliant. Clingon had said lots of things to me about how I was now his first choice of reserve and that I had a good attitude and how, miraculously, one of my two left feet had turned out all right. The more he praised me, the more I wanted to play, but I still wasn't comfortable being on court when Wills was in the team, and Wills had knuckled under and was behaving himself, so he was never going to be dropped. Anyway, he was easily the best and I didn't want him to be dropped.

'There's no point in worrying about it,' Penny

said. 'If you want to play, you'll have to leave it to your coach to decide when he puts you on, and if Wills is there at the same time you'll have to make the most of it.'

I knew she was right. The only way I could avoid playing with Wills was if I didn't play at all, and I wasn't going to drop out now.

'Surely it can't be that bad,' Penny continued. 'He can't do much with your coach watching. From what you've said, your coach won't take any nonsense from him.'

'He makes me feel as if I'm rubbish.'

'But you know you're not rubbish,' said Penny. 'You've just told me.'

'He doesn't pass to me unless he has to.' It sounded a bit pathetic.

'Everyone else will pass to you.'

Perhaps it was all in my mind. Perhaps I just felt overshadowed by Wills because he was so good.

'You'll be fine,' smiled Penny, 'if I know anything about anything.'

I sat down to do my maths and English homework, while Penny went off to catalogue a pile of new books. I started with maths to get it out of the way. The first five questions were easy, but I was stuck on question six when I saw a sudden movement out of the corner of my eye. I turned in the direction of the windows. I couldn't see anything through them, because the lower halves had that sort of frosted glass you get in bathrooms. I stared back down at my work, but another movement made me look round again. There was nothing there.

And then a hand popped up above the frosted glass and waggled its fingers, before disappearing. I waited. A few seconds later it happened again. *Jack*, I thought, *playing silly games*. I stood up and was about to walk over to the window, when four hands popped up and waggled their fingers.

Jack and a friend? He knew I didn't want him to tell anyone else about my hiding place. I would be livid with him if he had. The hands disappeared again. Perhaps it wasn't Jack at all. It was probably just kids mucking around. I sat down once more and tried to concentrate on question six.

A few moments passed before I was aware of another movement, but this time it was at the library door. I looked up, half expecting to see Jack after all, and ready to give him what-for if he was with somebody else.

It wasn't Jack. It was Wills's friends. They were sneaking in and heading round the shelves in my direction, while Penny was out the back unaware that anything was going on.

I thrust my maths book in front of my face, praying that they hadn't seen me. Of course they had. That's why they were there. They sat down on the other side of the table and the ginger one pulled the book away from my face.

'Well, if it isn't Big Willy's little brother,' he grinned.

'Did you like our puppet show?' smirked the dark one.

'Better than maths homework,' said the ginger one.

I looked beyond them in the hope that Penny would appear.

'Where is Big Willy today, anyway?'

I shrugged my shoulders. 'How should I know?' I muttered.

'Bit of a liability, your brother, isn't he?' the dark one smirked.

'Bit of a nutter,' added the other.

'Cracks us up though,' they both cackled.

If they thought I was going to agree with them, they'd have to wait a very long time.

'Let us down badly at the weekend, he did,' said the ginger one. 'Had it all set up to give him a good time and what happens? He doesn't show.'

'Maybe he had better things to do,' I muttered.

'Better than being with his friends when they've got such big plans for him?'

'I'm trying to work,' I said.

'Yeh, Big Willy says you're a bit of a swot.'

Just then Penny came out from the back room and glanced over in my direction. Wills's friends looked round at her and she came towards us.

'Friends of yours, Chris?' she said. 'New customers for me?'

I didn't know what to say, but one of Wills's friends looked her up and down and said, 'I wouldn't mind being one of your customers, darling. How much do you charge?'

The smile on Penny's face snapped shut. She looked questioningly at me and I dropped my eyes in embarrassment.

'Would you like to leave my library now?' she ordered.

'We haven't finished here yet.'

'We need to find a book on the mating habits of sea lions.'

'Yeh. No blubbering, Chris.'

They fell about laughing as if they had cracked the greatest joke in the world. I wanted to smack the silly grins off their faces, instead I sat there feeling useless.

'I asked you to leave,' said Penny calmly.

'What if we don't want to?'

'Then I shall call the police.'

'But we ain't done nothing.'

'I'm not arguing,' said Penny. 'Are you going to leave, or am I going to have you thrown out?'

Just then a man walked in carrying a bundle of

books under his arm. He looked across at us and waved at Penny.

'Good afternoon, Penny,' he said and pointed to the books. 'I'll leave them on the counter, shall I, while I choose something else?'

'Of course, Mr Clayton,' she replied. 'I'll be with you right away.'

'Nice to see some youngsters in here,' he said. 'Catch the reading habit early.'

'Nice to see some wrinklies in here,' smirked the ginger one. 'Keep them off the streets.'

They howled with laughter again. Penny was furious. She turned in the direction of the telephone and was about to pick it up, when they both stood up.

'Nice to meet you, Penny,' the dark one said. 'We've taken up enough of your time.'

And then, as they approached the door, he continued, 'Don't worry though, we'll be back.'

They turned and skipped out, leaping up to waggle their fingers above the frosted glass as they went. I breathed a sigh of relief, but my chest was still pounding.

'Are you all right?' Penny asked. I nodded.

'Who were they?'

'Wills's friends.'

'I thought so,' said Penny. 'Nice choice.'

She went off to serve Mr Clayton, who observed that they weren't her usual sort of customer, and to make a cup of tea. While she was away, I realised that my hiding place had been discovered, that I had become a problem for Penny, and that I would never be able to go there again. However much Penny reassured me that she would deal with it if Wills's friends ever came back, I would never be able to relax, and neither would she.

CHAPTER SEVENTEEN

The rest of the week was agony before the Saturday of the tournament arrived. I wandered the streets after school, rather than go home and risk being stuck on my own with Wills. I didn't want to see him. He might not have been in the library that day, but what had happened was still his fault. They were his friends. Wills didn't say anything about it, but I was sure his friends would have enjoyed telling him that they had found me swotting IN THE LIBRARY and what a complete saddo that made me. Mum kept asking me what was wrong and why was I so grumpy, but I just shrugged my shoulders and said it was nothing, so she gave up in the end.

The only way I could do my homework was if I shut myself up in my room and turned on my music. Even then I could still hear Mum arguing with Wills about not doing his work, about complaints from school, about going out, about staying out, about swearing, about having the telly on too loud, about dribbling and slamming and dunking anything he could lay his hands on. You'd think I would be used to it, but you try blocking out a hurricane, especially if you're worried someone is getting hurt in it, or if you're expecting your door to come crashing in at any moment.

During the night before the tournament, Wills came into my room and woke me up.

'You don't like me, do you?' he said.

'Not when you wake me up in the middle of the night, I don't,' I muttered.

'No, but you don't anyway, do you?'

'Why do you expect me to like you when you're horrible to me,' I said.

'What if I was nice to you, then?'

'Try it,' I sighed. 'What's this all about, Wills?'

'I don't mean all the things I do.' He sounded sort of defeated.

'What, like you didn't mean to send me all those nasty text messages?'

'It was just a bit of fun.'

Surely even Wills couldn't believe that!

'Only for you and your stupid friends,' I said.

'They're not stupid,' Wills mumbled.

'They're stupid and ugly and horrible and you know it,' I growled.

'Just cos they caught you being a saddo in the library,' Wills said.

'I knew you'd say that. Why don't you just leave me alone?'

'I really need you to be there for me tomorrow,' Wills said quietly. 'I mean, will you shout at me if I start to cock up? I need you to be on my side, Chris, because some of them other kids are waiting for me to cock up big time, I know it. They're gonna try and make me cock up so that I get chucked out of the team, like last time. I promise I'll listen to you.'

I couldn't understand why Wills was so sure

that the other kids were out to get him, and why he didn't think that Clingon would deal with it. But then I didn't understand half of what went on in Wills's head.

'I need you to be on my side too,' I said. 'It's your fault your friends won't leave me alone.'

'I didn't know you went to the library. That wasn't my fault,' protested Wills.

'I won't go there any more,' I said.

'I'll tell them to leave you alone, then,' said Wills. 'I'll tell them to leave you alone or they'll have me to answer to.'

'Scary,' I scoffed.

'You can laugh,' said Wills huffily, 'but what I say goes with them. They respect me, and they'll do whatever I tell them.'

I stared at Wills and could see that he really believed what he was saying. I didn't believe it for a minute, not even for a second.

'You never ever pass to me when I'm playing at the same time as you,' I said accusingly.

'I promise I'll pass to you, all the time,' Wills said.

'Even when I'm on the bench?' I grinned. I wanted to lighten the mood now.

'On the bench?' bellowed Wills. 'I won't let them leave you on the bench! You're my brother. Where I go, you go!'

'Together we stand!' I shouted.

'Divided — we fall!' shouted Wills, and he dropped like a pillar of stone on to my bed.

'Ow, you plonker, that hurt,' I yelled, 'and you've woken Muffin up.'

'Sorry, Muffin,' chuckled Wills. 'Sorry, bruv.'

He giddy-upped back to his bedroom, leaving me to rub my elbowed chest to the rattle of Muffin on his wheel.

I felt lousy the next morning, tired and knotted up with nerves. It had taken me ages to get to sleep after Wills's night-time visit, and I sat at the breakfast table, yawning my head off. Wills was subdued too. I wondered if it was because he was tired, or because he was nervous, or both. Mum was excited. She chatted away about how much she was looking forward to watching us. She wanted us to teach her the rules of basketball, because she had never even seen a match before. I tried to explain, with Wills interrupting me to tell me when I'd got it wrong, and I think we left her totally confused.

'I expect I shall pick it up,' she said.

Wills snorted. 'It's a well-known fact that women are rubbish at anything to do with sport,' he said.

'It's a well-known fact that teenagers are incredibly patronising and think they know everything,' retorted Mum. 'You keep your generalisations to yourself, young man.'

'Keep your hair on, Mumsy-wumsy, I was only joking,' Wills grinned. 'But you are the weaker sex, aren't you?'

Mum tried to swat him across the kitchen table and knocked over her cup of coffee.

'Now look what you've made me do,' she groaned.

'Clumsy-mumsy,' Wills scolded. Then, for the hundredth time he asked, 'How long is it till we go?'

The tournament was being held in the local leisure centre. Dad was coming to collect us all at half past twelve and we were due to have a practice at the centre before the tournament started at half past one. It was a relief when at last he arrived. 'How's the dream team, then?' he asked, standing on the doorstep, freshly shaved, skittle body crammed into a tracksuit and trainers. 'All fit and raring to go?'

'Cor blimey, Dad,' said Wills. 'Anyone would think you were our coach.'

'Just like to get into the mood,' said Dad.

'Well, you only just got into those trousers,' guffawed Wills.

Dad took a playful swipe at him, then took Mum by the elbow and steered her out of the house.

'Come on, you two, let's show them how it's really done.'

Anyone would think he was playing as well, I thought.

It felt peculiar to be in the back seat of the car next to Wills, with Mum and Dad in the front just like old times, except that Wills didn't bash me, or lie on me, and Mum and Dad talked to each other like they didn't know each other very well, which I suppose they didn't any more. Wills got a text on his mobile phone. He looked at me to see if I was trying to read it. I wasn't and I turned away, but out of the corner of my eye I could see him texting back with urgent thumbs. Another text came straight back and after he had answered it again he snapped the phone shut and shoved it in his pocket. He left it to rumble there and I wondered why he didn't want to see what the messages were.

When we arrived at the leisure centre, it was packed with boys from other teams, all wearing different colours and slamming and dunking wherever they could find a bit of space. The noise was ear-splitting, but the excitement was catching and the butterflies in my stomach became more like enthusiastic bees. Wills looked startled at first and stood behind me, but then he spotted Clingon and pushed past me to announce himself. Mum and Dad patted me on the back and wished me good luck, before going off for a coffee and to find seats in the spectators' gallery.

It was good to have a warm-up before the tournament started. Clingon found a corner of the hall and made us do some drills, then he made us huddle together for a team talk, which ended with us all yelling JUST WATCH US FLY! at the tops of our voices.

We weren't playing in the first match, so we sat on benches at the side to watch and 'suss out the opposition' as Clingon put it. Wills couldn't stop fidgeting. I didn't blame him, because all the waiting was turning the bees back into butterflies again. Both the teams in the first match seemed to be too good for us, and I was sure we would be trounced. But Wills turned to me and said loudly that they were a load of donkeys and we could beat them with our boxers round our ankles. Then his mobile phone went off. He pulled it out of his jog bottoms and read the message. His face went white and he slammed it shut. Then he opened it again and sent a text. When the reply came, Clingon glared at him and told him to turn it off or else. Wills read the message, slammed the phone shut again and threw it into his bag. He saw me looking at him and stuck his tongue out, but he didn't go back to watching the match. He was biting his fingernails and his leg was twitching up and down while he stared round the hall.

Suddenly he jumped to his feet, yelling, 'I need the bog!' and rushed off in the direction of the toilets.

'Don't be long,' Clingon shouted after him. 'We're on in a minute.'

Wills didn't reply. He disappeared through a door and a few seconds later the whistle blew for the end of the first match. Clingon told us to jog up and down the court while the other teams drifted off, then called us together for a final team talk.

'Where's that brother of yours got to?' he asked irritably.

'Shall I go and see if he's all right?' I replied.

'Be quick about it.'

I ran across the hall, glancing up to see if Mum and Dad were watching. They waved, not realising that anything was the matter. I raised my hand, but kept on running through the door Wills had taken, past some stairs and into the gents toilets.

'Wills,' I called, 'hurry up, we're on!'

There was no reply. The doors to two of the cubicles were shut. I called again, but there was still no reply. One of the doors opened but the boy who came out wasn't Wills. I stood impatiently by the other door and hissed, 'Wills, stop messing around and come out. You've been in there ages.'

There was a loud fart, which convinced me that it was Wills, but when the door eventually opened another boy came out, grinned at me and said, 'Wrong person, mate,' before loping off back to the hall.

Wills was nowhere to be seen. I checked the disabled toilet next door, because it would have been just like Wills to go in there and pull the red cord, and I ran up the stairs, which led to another part of the building that was obviously out of bounds. There was no sign of him. On the way back down the stairs I met TJ, who was one of the other reserves.

'What the hell are you doing, Chris, and

where's Wills?' he shouted. 'Clingon's doing his nut out there.'

'I can't find him!' I cried.

'Typical,' groaned TJ. 'Trust your brother to let us down.'

'He was worried about playing,' I said rather lamely.

'We were all worried about him playing,' TJ snapped. 'You'd better get back in there quick, and tell Clingon what's happened.'

As I went back through the doors, the whistle blew for the start of our match. I made my way round the side of the court and glanced up again at Mum and Dad. They knew something was wrong this time. Dad mouthed: 'Where's Wills?' and I shrugged my shoulders. He spoke to Mum and they both began to scour the hall. As I reached Clingon, who was shouting instructions across the court, I saw Dad get up and make for the doors to the toilets.

'I can't find him, Mr Columbine,' I said nervously. 'I think he might have been too scared to play.'

'Well, he'd better be too scared to come back

into this hall,' Clingon growled, 'because if I get my hands on him he'll learn a new meaning for slam-dunk.'

I sat down on the bench and saw Dad come back shaking his head. After a quick word with Mum, he strode off in the direction of the entrance to the leisure centre. We were already ten points down by then. Clingon told me he was putting me on. I didn't want to go on. Not without Wills there. This was his big day, and he'd blown it, and I felt sorry for him. And then I felt angry. So angry. This was my day as well and Wills was wrecking it. Dad wasn't there to watch me because of Wills, because of Wills and his stupid Acts Daft and Dumb. I wanted so badly for Dad to be there with Mum, but instead he was rushing around trying to find Wills.

'Will you get on there now!' Clingon shouted at me. 'It's enough that one of you can't do as you're told.'

In my dreams, I would have been the hero of the hour. We would have been losing and I would have taken the match by the scruff of its neck and turned it around. I would have been lifted high in the air, and everyone would have cheered until they were hoarse. But this was no dream. This was a nightmare. I went on the court and I was useless. An embarrassment. I could see Mum trying to be all proud and cheering when I managed to make my first interception, but she kept looking around to see if she could see Dad and Wills. Gradually she slumped back in her seat, as my fingers turned to butter and my feet fought each other to play on the left. Then Dad reappeared, on his own. Clingon was patient and encouraging to begin with, but it was a relief for everyone when at last he sent me back to the bench, with the match already dead and buried, and me as well.

There was a break before our next match. Clingon let me go and talk to Mum and Dad. I couldn't help it, but I started blubbing when I sat with them. I felt like I'd let everyone down. Mum said she was proud of me and that she'd seen me do lots of good things. I said I was upset about Wills, not just because I'd played like a fairy. Dad said that I was to stop worrying about Wills and that it was Wills's choice to run away. He should have stayed and faced his fears like everyone else, because everyone else would have been nervous too. Mum said Dad was being unfair. Wills had a lot to deal with, what with his Acts Daft and Dumb and everyone expecting more of him because he was big for his age. Dad said she shouldn't always make excuses for him. Mum began to get upset because she said that he had a good heart but his head sometimes told him to do the wrong thing. Some people behind us told us to shush because they were trying to watch the match, and I thought Dad was going to say something rude to them. Instead he said I should go back and get ready for our next match, and that they would worry about Wills later.

'Go on, Chris, get out there and show them who's who,' Dad urged.

I said I'd try, but I didn't really feel like it and I didn't think Clingon would let me near the court again. Clingon took me aside for a talk and told me to forget about Wills and concentrate on my own game, otherwise I would be sitting on the bench for the rest of the afternoon.

I did play better in our next match, when Clingon eventually put me on, but I wasn't great and the team missed Wills's strength. We lost again, and only managed to scrape a narrow win in our final match. That meant that we didn't go through to the semi-finals, and I had to sit there and listen while the other boys bad-mouthed Wills for letting them down. Clingon didn't say much, but I could tell he was annoyed and I guessed that he wouldn't exactly welcome Wills or me to his next Sunday session.

Mum and Dad came over to console me and to apologise to Clingon for Wills's vanishing act. We headed off home then, me on my own in the back seat, Mum and Dad in front, just like old times, except that we didn't know where Wills was, and Mum and Dad weren't really talking to each other because Mum thought Dad was too hard on Wills and Dad thought Mum was too soft. We were all sure that Wills would be at home sulking when we got there. He wasn't though. The house was empty and there was no sign that Wills had been back and gone out again. Dad hovered on the doorstep, looking uncomfortable. Mum told him to come in, and she would put the kettle on.

'He's always going off for hours on end,' she said, but I could tell she was anxious.

'Do you want me to wait with you until he comes back?' Dad asked, as we sat at the kitchen table.

Mum nodded, but after he had finished his cup of tea he stood up and said he was going to have a scout around. Mum began to busy herself with preparing food, and I went to see the football results on the telly. I was tired and fed up. Our big day had been a big disaster. Not just on the basketball court. I realised that, like Wills, I had been harbouring a tiny hope that Mum and Dad might just get together again as they shared the glory of our basketball triumph, however daft that might sound. Now I understood that they were further apart than ever, but it had nothing to do with what had happened.

Dad came back and said that Wills was nowhere to be seen. I could feel the anxiety mounting, even though it still wasn't very late.

'That boy will be the death of me,' Dad said.

Mum burst into tears and then got cross with herself for being silly. I couldn't stand just sitting there any longer, even though there was a big match starting soon on the telly. I jumped up and said that I was going out on my bike to have a look for him. I left Dad trying to comfort Mum, but he wasn't very good at it any more.

CHAPTER EIGHTEEN

It felt good to be out on my bike, whistling along the road down to the canal, away from the tension at home, away from the tension of the day. I wanted the wind to sweep up all the bad things into an enormous gigantic sack, and hurl it into space. In it would be me being rubbish at basketball, the tournament, Mum being cross with Dad, Dad being cross with Mum, Mum and Dad not being together, Wills's horrible friends, the money under Wills's mattress, the knife wherever it was, Wills finding my story, and Wills's Acts Daft and Dumb.

I was sure I would find Wills with his friends. If I found him, I was going to cycle up, tell him Mum and Dad were worried about him, then cycle away again as quickly as possible before his friends could say or do anything horrible. If I found him, at least I would be able to go home and tell Mum and Dad that he was all right. Then they could stop worrying, Dad would be able to go back to his own home, and Mum and I could sit down and watch the telly together like we normally did when Wills was out.

I couldn't find Wills though. I searched all of his usual haunts twice over, in case he was on the move from one to the other. I was about to give up and go home, when I remembered the scrapyard, and the time when I thought I had seen him coming out of the scrap merchant's building. It was worth a try.

I cycled there as fast as I could, because it was beginning to get dark. The scrapyard was empty, probably because of the match on the telly and because it was nearly teatime for most people. It wasn't the sort of place I wanted to be on my own. In the gloom, the scrap merchant's building looked spooky and unwelcoming. The danger signs with their white backgrounds shouted their message out louder than ever. I couldn't believe anyone would want to go inside, even on the brightest, sunniest day. I laid my bike down on the ground and walked slowly over, ready to turn round and run if Wills's friends suddenly appeared. I stood outside the building and listened. I couldn't hear anything, and it didn't look possible to get in through the heavily barricaded doors. Perhaps I had been wrong about Wills and his friends coming from inside the building. Perhaps they had just been walking by.

I went round to the back. There was another set of doors, padlocked and with large planks of wood across them. I reached through the planks and rattled the doors half-heartedly, knowing already that they would not give way. I felt defeated and relieved at the same time.

I turned to go home, when I noticed a small door to the right, set back into the brickwork and fastened with a padlock and a criss-cross of narrow slats of wood. Some of these were broken lower down, leaving a gap large enough for a person to crawl through, if they were stupid enough to want to. And then I noticed that the padlock was not locking anything together. It was hanging from a hook, but behind it the door was slightly ajar. I put my hand through the slats and pushed the door gently. It squeaked on its hinges and the bottom dragged on the ground, but it gave way a little. I listened for any sounds from inside. Nothing.

DANGER! the signs warned me. I was sure there was nobody there, but curiosity made me hesitate to go away. DANGER! DANGER!

Then I heard something move. My first instinct was to leg it. My second was that it might only be a rat. My third was that if Wills was in there with his horrible friends, I wanted to know what they were doing. I'd had enough of all the secrecy. I'd had enough of his friends interfering in my life. I'd had enough of his friends full stop. What could they do to me if I did barge in on them, except call me more rude names? At least if Wills knew I knew whatever it was he was up to, he might think twice about carrying on with it, especially if I said I was definitely going to tell Mum and Dad.

I squatted down and pushed gently again at the door, cursing because it squealed at every nudge and gave away the fact that I was there. I steeled myself to come face to face with a welcoming party as I crawled on my hands and knees through the gap. I stood up to find that on the other side of the door a narrow concrete staircase rose steeply to an upper floor. I waited at the bottom for a few seconds and listened, trying to blot out the whooshing of blood in my head. There was no sound. I crept up the first three steps, but hesitated again. My nerve was deserting me. Why was I putting myself through this? I didn't have to. Why didn't I just make up my mind that there was nobody there and go home?

Something flashed past my face, and I screamed.

A pigeon landed behind me and fled through the door. I became aware of several more pigeons scrabbling around above me, and saw piles of their droppings on the steps ahead.

Then I heard a different sound. It was like someone sobbing. I took a deep breath and whispered, 'Who's there?'

'Don't hurt me,' a voice cried back.

'Wills?' I said.

The sobs increased. I climbed to the top of the steps, ducking to avoid the sheets of cobwebs which hung from the rafters.

A huge room opened up before me. The darkness was broken only by patches of light where the roof had caved in. Sinister-looking shapes seemed to move around in the gloom, but I saw that they were only pieces of scrap metal that had been left lying there. The sobs were coming from the other end of the room. I walked slowly towards them, the floorboards creaking and groaning under my feet.

'Wills?' I said.

I moved forward again, until I could make out Wills's face. He was cowering in a corner, shaking uncontrollably.

'What are you doing, Wills? What's happened?'

Wills howled now, his whole body heaving. It

was frightening. I didn't know what to do to make him stop. If only I'd had my mobile with me I could have rung Mum or Dad.

'Where's your mobile, Wills?' I asked. 'Let me ring Mum.'

He shook his head miserably. I didn't understand what that was supposed to mean. And then I remembered that he had thrown it into his kit bag.

'Come on, Wills,' I said. 'Whatever it is, it can't be that bad.'

At last, he whimpered, 'It is that bad. It's worse than bad.'

'What is? Tell me, Wills.'

'I'm going to go to prison.'

The words leapt around inside my head as I tried to make sense of them.

'What are you talking about?' I spluttered.

'When they find out I was there, they'll send me to prison.'

'Don't be daft, Wills. Nobody's going to send you to prison,' I said.

Why did everything have to be such a drama? I thought.

'They didn't tell me they were going to do the library. I didn't want to do it, Chris, but they made me go with them.'

He started to sob again. Suddenly I felt as if my insides were being squeezed tight by an iron fist.

'I hate them,' howled Wills. He shrank back further into the corner. 'They might come and get me. I ran away. They said they'd come and get me if I ran away.'

'Your friends?' I whispered.

'They're not my friends,' he wailed. 'I hate them. They threatened that woman with a knife.'

This was no drama. This was for real. Even Wills couldn't make this up. I wanted to laugh and cry and be sick all at the same time. I was losing control. This was my brother talking about my friend. A knife, he said. THE KNIFE. I wanted to run away, to get out of that place, and be at home sitting on the settee with Mum. I wished this was just a bad dream so that I could wake up in the morning and everything would be like it was every day, with Mum clattering away downstairs and hippo snorts coming from Wills' bedroom.

'They said we were just going to frighten her because she's a stuck-up cow and deserves it. I didn't know they were going to use a knife. I didn't know they were going to trash the place.'

I was angry then. I could feel it boiling up inside me like a volcano.

'She isn't a stuck-up cow,' I raged at him. 'She's my friend. What have you done?'

I started to pummel him with my fists.

'Why do you have to ruin everything, EVERY-THING?' I yelled.

I wanted to hurt him so badly. He tried to protect himself with his arms, while he begged me to stop.

Then the hurricane broke through. He yelled at the top of his voice, 'LEAVE ME ALONE. IT WASN'T MY FAULT!'

At the same time, he pushed me with all his might, hurling me backwards like one of those crash-test dummies.

I went straight through the rotten floorboards.

For a moment there was silence.

Shocked silence.

Then the pain hit me like a blow from a hammer, and Wills's voice cried hysterically from above, 'Chris, are you all right, Chris, oh God, please let him be all right, please don't let him be dead!'

I lifted my head to speak, but the only sound I could make was a loud moan from deep in my throat. I saw that my right leg was twisted sideways. I knew straightaway it was broken. I'd seen footballers with broken legs on the telly. I tried to be brave like they were, because the funny thing is that if footballers are really, *really* hurt they don't make a fuss. It's only when they're being prima donnas or want to get another player into trouble or want to make the referee point to the penalty spot, that they roll around as if they're about to die. I didn't think I was about to die, even if the pain was worse than any pain I had ever felt in my life. But I was scared, and I wanted Mum.

'Chris?'

Wills's voice was panic-stricken. I heard a low

wail and thought it was him, until I realised it had come from my own lips. There was a scuffling sound up above.

'Wills,' I cried, summoning all my strength, 'keep away from the hole, Wills! Don't come near the hole.'

'I thought you were dead,' he howled. 'I didn't mean it, Chris. I didn't mean any of it.'

'I think I've broken my leg, Wills. You need to get help.'

'I can't go outside,' he said. 'They might get me.'

He was terrified, I could hear it in his voice.

'There's nobody there, Wills.'

'I want to stay here with you. Please don't make me go.'

I heard him moving around again. I was scared that he might fall through the floor and hurt himself, even more badly than I'd been hurt. But I was relieved that he didn't want to go, because I didn't want to be left on my own however much I wanted Mum.

'It hurts, Wills,' I groaned. 'Keep talking to me.

Tell me things so I don't have to think about the pain.'

There was a silence before he said, 'I don't want to talk about what happened, all right? I don't want to remember it.'

I didn't either.

'We lost the basketball,' I said. 'I was rubbish.'

There was silence again, and I thought Wills might not want to talk about the basketball because he would know it was his fault we lost.

'You're not rubbish,' he said then, quietly, and I think he really meant it. 'You just need to grow a bit. I'm lucky cos I'm big.'

'Sometimes you're unlucky being big, because people think you're older than you are and expect you to behave older.'

'Dad's like that,' said Wills. 'He thinks I should act older.'

'And Mum sometimes babies you,' I said.

'I suppose Clingon is furious with me,' Wills sighed.

'I don't think you're his favourite.'

'I'd like to be a basketballer when I'm grown up.'

'I'd like to be a writer,' I said, and immediately wished I hadn't.

'So you can write about me, I suppose,' Wills threw down.

'Been there, done that, got the torn pages,' I threw back. 'You're not the only subject in the world.'

'I'm the only one worth writing about,' said Wills. I could hear the chuckle in his voice and was glad.

We both fell silent for a time. Thoughts of Penny kept breaking through, even though I was trying to keep them buried. I was beginning to feel dizzy with pain and fear and hunger. As if he could read my mind, Wills suddenly said, 'I could murder a pizza.'

'They don't deliver here,' I groaned.

Wills chuckled again. 'You're quite funny sometimes,' he said.

'Thanks for the vote,' I muttered.

'Does it hurt much?' Wills sounded anxious again.

'It hurts like hell,' I said, 'but I'll live, no thanks to you.'

And then, in a flash, it hit me. Penny didn't work on Saturdays. Someone else did. If anyone had been hurt, it wasn't Penny.

I felt so relieved, and then I felt guilty about feeling relieved, because it meant that the girl who worked on Saturdays was the girl who had been threatened.

I had to be sure. 'Wills?' I called.

'Yes, bruv,' said Wills.

'What did she look like, the girl in the library?'

'Don't want to talk about it,' he snapped.

'Did she have dark hair?' I persisted.

'No. I don't know. I don't think so. Leave it alone, will you?'

We went quiet again. I could hear Wills shifting around. I didn't know which would be worse: his thoughts, with the knowing what had happened; or my thoughts, with not knowing what had happened, and trying not to fear the worst. It was pitch-black now, and I was beginning to shiver. I closed my eyes, but I was scared I wouldn't wake up again, and I wanted to see Mum. I wanted to see Mum more than anything else in the world. She would make everything all right again. That's what mums do, isn't it?

'Chris?' Wills called. 'When are they going to find us?

'I don't know,' I sighed. I didn't want to think about it. Someone would come eventually, but the thought of being there all night terrified me. 'Mum and Dad will be worried. I expect they'll call the police.'

'No!' cried Wills. 'I don't want the police! They'll send me to prison! Don't let the police take me, Chris. Tell them it wasn't me.'

He was becoming so agitated that the floor was beginning to creak.

'Keep still, Wills. Stay in the corner!' I yelled.

'Promise you won't let them take me away,' he wailed.

'I won't let them take you away, Wills,' I promised. 'You're my brother.'

'Together we stand?' he shouted.

'Divided we fall.' I grimaced.

I had fallen, badly, and we were divided not just by a rotten floor, but by what Wills had been through that day, which I couldn't even begin to understand, and which threatened all of us. Just like Dad leaving had threatened all of us. Still threatened all of us. We weren't the same any more. Could we somewhere, somehow, discover a different sort of togetherness when all of this was over?

CHAPTER NINETEEN

I must have drifted off to sleep, because the next thing I knew was that someone was rattling the door and I had the daft idea that I was supposed to shout, 'Come in!' The pain from my leg hit me like a bolt of lightning, and my chest felt as if someone had jumped on it.

'Wills?' I called.

There was no reply.

I heard a scuffling sound, and a dog barked.

'Wills?' I called again. There was still no answer and I guessed he must be asleep.

I heard voices and the noise of wood snapping. The door scraped on the ground. The dog barked again. Heavy boots thudded on the steps. The pigeons flapped.

'Christopher?' a man called.

I saw a light dart around the room above and hover over the hole. A dog barked excitedly.

'I'm down here,' I called.

'It's all right, son, it's the police,' the man said. 'Stay where you are, just stay there.'

I'm not going anywhere, I thought to myself.

A woman's voice continued, 'There's nothing to be frightened of. We just want to get you back home. Are you on your own?'

'Wills is in the corner up there,' I called. 'You have to be kind to him, it wasn't his fault.'

'Wills is safe and sound outside with your parents,' the woman said. 'He told us you were here.'

What did she mean? How could Wills have told them? He didn't have his mobile with him.

Someone began to shuffle slowly across the floorboards. They creaked loudly, sending down showers of dust.

'It's too dangerous,' the man's voice said. 'Christopher? Are you all right, lad?'

I tried to answer, but it was like my voice had been banged out of me. A loud groan was as much as I could produce.

'We'll have to break in downstairs, lad. Just hold on tight, all right?'

I nodded in the dark and let my head flop back on the ground. I felt so relieved. It was over. Someone else was taking charge. I could hear the police talking up above, making arrangements to get me out. I would see Mum and Dad again soon. I bet Wills was glad that it wasn't his horrible friends who had found him, even if he was scared stiff that the police would lock him away. And then I realised that it wasn't all over for Wills. It had only just begun. When they broke through to where I was lying, I wanted to be awake enough to tell them that it wasn't his fault.

The rest was a blur. There was a lot of banging and sirens and more voices and walkie-talkies and waves of dust and cobwebs and great gasps of air, when the doors gave way, and paramedics lifting me and Mum hugging me and Dad saying all right son and Wills leaning over me, saying: 'I did it,

Chris, I went and got help,' and the bright light in the ambulance and the drip in my arm and Mum holding my hand, while Dad listened to Wills talking and realised that it wasn't all over.

CHAPTER TWENTY

I lay on the hard hospital bed, my right leg in plaster to halfway up my thigh, my chest strapped because I'd broken three ribs, and stitches underneath a wad of bandage on my other leg where I'd gashed it.

'You won't be playing football for a while, then,' observed Jack.

'I could beat you one-legged, no problem,' I said.

'In your dreams,' he retorted. 'I got picked for captain even though my best friend didn't help me practise.'

'Shows you didn't need me, then,' I shrugged.

'It's only your biscuits I'm after,' he laughed,

and grabbed one from a packet on my bedside table. 'Still no choccy ones, I see. Talking of which, has that Penny been in to see you?'

I nodded. 'She's the one who brought the biscuits.'

'How's her mate?' Jack asked.

'She's going to be all right.'

'Lucky for Wills, eh?'

'It wasn't his fault,' I said quickly, and for the hundredth time. 'They told him all he had to do was keep an eye on the caretaker out the back. He thought they were just going to scare her and see if she had any money. I know that's bad enough, but he didn't know they were going to use a knife. He didn't know they were going to trash the place.'

'It's been in the newspaper,' said Jack, 'about thugs causing fifty thousand pounds' worth of damage and threatening the librarian with a knife.'

'Did it mention Wills?'

Jack shook his head. 'But there was another piece about brothers William and Christopher Jennings larking around in a dangerous building, and Christopher falling through the floor.'

I groaned. Mum and Dad would have hated that. I hated that.

'Wills went to fetch help, even though he was terrified those thugs would get him for running away,' I said.

'So Wills is a hero now,' Jack smirked.

'Course he's not,' I said, 'but at least he tried to do something to put things right.'

'So he should, after what he did to you.'

'Wills is the one who's got hurt the most,' I murmured.

'You're the one who's got hurt the most,' argued Jack.

'Only my body,' I said. 'Not my head.'

I knew as I said it that it was more than that. We had all been hurt. Mum and Dad were tearing themselves and each other apart trying to work out where they had gone wrong, what they could have done better, why they hadn't taken enough notice of the warning signs that Wills was running off the rails. They kept saying sorry to me that they hadn't protected me more. I kept saying sorry to them that I hadn't told them more about Wills's horrible friends and the knife and the money under the bed, money which his horrible friends had given him for distracting onlookers while they used the knife to frighten shopkeepers into opening their tills. Wills kept running around like a headless chicken saying sorry to everyone, but it didn't stop him having to spend hours down at the police station explaining exactly what he had been up to over the past few months.

'Wouldn't make any difference to Wills's head,' sniggered Jack. 'He's a nutter anyway.'

'Only I'm allowed to say that,' I said sharply. 'Anyway, he's not a nutter. He's just – Wills, that's all.'

'You can say what you like,' said Jack. 'I'm glad he's not my brother.'

I'd had enough then. I wanted Jack to go away. It was all a bit of a laugh for him, a bit of entertainment. It wasn't for me, and it wasn't for Wills. Mum had told me that Wills was in serious trouble. He might not have been the one to threaten the librarian, but he was an accessory, whatever that was, and he admitted that he had been looking after the knife for his friends. He admitted, too, that he had been shoplifting with them.

'What's going to happen to him?' Jack asked.

'Don't know,' I said. 'I'm tired. I want to go to sleep now.'

I did know. Mum had told me that the police had cautioned Wills, and that if he got into trouble again he could expect the consequences to be serious. He was going to have to change schools, because our school wouldn't have him back after what he had done. They said they had done their best for him, but that perhaps it was time for him to make a fresh start somewhere else.

'Wills will hate that,' I said. 'He hates going anywhere where he has to meet new people who don't know about his Acts Daft and Dumb.'

'Don't call it that,' Mum said sharply. 'You're not to call it that. Anyway, he doesn't have a lot of choice. And we've got you to consider as well.' She began to get tearful. 'You said yourself that you're fed up with being relied on and want to do normal boy things. I should have understood more what you were going through. Now it's time to put you first.'

That made me really upset. It was like Wills was being sent to a new school because of me, even if he would have had to go anyway. I should have been happy that at least for part of my days I would be living in a hurricane-free zone where no one could lump me together with him. But I couldn't be happy because I was sad for Wills, even when Mum told me that the school was much smaller, and had teachers who could look after Wills better.

Wills came to see me every day. At first he was very subdued and I spent the whole time trying to cheer him up. He kept saying sorry, until I wanted to shove a sock in his mouth to stop him. Mum said that he had gone berserk when they told him about changing schools. He said he would run away rather than have to put up with a new load of donkeys. Then he got all clingy and said he would superglue himself to Mum. When he told me they did basketball, and had an enormous swimming pool, and a floodlit soccer pitch, I said he must be mad if he didn't want to go there.

One afternoon, Wills came bouncing in and leapt on my bed.

'Careful, you dolt!' I yelped. 'You nearly broke my other leg.'

'Sorry, bruv,' he said. 'Just thought you'd like to know that you're talking to a genuine brain-box.'

'Oh, yeh, who says?'

'I've done the tests, haven't I? You know, like the ones I had to do when I was younger, but these were a lot lot harder. Those psychologist types made me do them to see if I had a screw loose, but I haven't. Dad couldn't believe it,' he guffawed. 'You can kiss my feet if you like.'

'You can kiss my butt,' I flung back. 'Doesn't mean you can't be stupid.'

'I could become Prime Minister,' he said airily.

'Pigs might fly,' I snorted.

'You'll miss me when you can't see me every day at school.'

'Like a hole in the head.'

Wills went round the ward, chatting loudly to the other patients and nurses and anyone else he could find. He picked up patients' notes and pretended to be a surgeon about to perform an operation on each one of them in turn, until one of the nurses shooed him away. I pulled the pillow over my head and wanted to die of embarrassment, but I was glad that Wills was happier, even if it was at my expense.

He came back and bounced on the bed again. 'I bet you're jealous that I'm going to a better school than you?' he asked.

'Who says it's better?'

'Stands to reason if it's got a floodlit soccer pitch and a swimming pool and basketball,' he said.

'I don't like swimming, and I'm no good at basketball, and the football pitch at our school is OK, plus I won't be doing sport for a while, plus my friends are there,' I replied.

'They're all donkeys at that school,' scoffed Wills. 'I don't know how you'll put up with them once I've gone.'

'I'll be all right, thanks for your concern.'

Wills went all thoughtful, before saying quietly, 'I'm scared, bruv. What if nobody likes me at the new school? What if they get fed up with me like they did at the old school?'

I didn't really know how to answer that, because it was true that all the other kids got fed up with Wills, and you couldn't blame them.

'What if I cock up again?' he carried on. 'I mean, if I cock up again the police or those psychologist types might say I have to be sent away.'

'No one's going to send you away, Wills,' I said, trying to reassure him.

'But they will if I do like I did before.'

'You won't though, will you?' I said. 'You won't be seeing your horrible friends again, and Mum and Dad and your new teachers are going to make sure you don't get into trouble.'

'But I can't help getting into trouble.' His leg was jerking up and down wildly and he was biting his nails.'

'Nobody expects you never to get into trouble again,' I grinned.

'Don't they?' He sounded surprised.

'Course not,' I laughed. 'That would take a miracle.'

'Miracles happen,' Wills retorted snottily. 'You just wait and see.'

CHAPTER TWENTY-ONE

A miracle hasn't happened, surprise surprise, but the hurricanes aren't quite so strong and don't happen quite so often – though they are still bad enough when they do. I think that what went on that day in the library, and in the scrapyard, frightened Wills so much that warning signals began to sound in his head if he started to lose control. It didn't stop him trying to knock me off my crutches or calling me Stumpy, but mostly he was nicer to me and even went to fetch things for me, if I couldn't carry them because of the crutches.

The best thing is that Wills gets home from school a lot later than me. His new school is further away and they make everyone stay to do their homework. (Why do they call it homework if they do it at school?) Twice a week he stays after homework to play basketball. That means that I can come home from school and be on my own and do what I wanted without interruption. Sometimes Jack or my other friends (I seem to have more now that Wills isn't there to put them off) come back to play on the computer or watch the telly.

Even Mum gets home before Wills. If I'm already back, I make her a cup of tea and we sit down at the kitchen table with a plate of biscuits and talk about how our days have been. I've found out so much about Mum's work that I didn't know before because there was never a chance to ask, and she's amazed that I'm thinking about being a writer, even though she knows I like to read and had thought about entering that competition.

'You'll have to show me what you write,' she smiled. 'I'd like to read it.'

'Nothing I've written has been good enough

yet,' I said grimly. 'It's so hard to come up with ideas.'

'I'm sure if you put your mind to it you'll get there in the end,' she said. 'Let's see some of that determination I know you've got.'

'It's better now, isn't it, Mum?' I said. 'It's like everything's calmed down a bit.'

It's Dad's job to pick up Wills in the morning because the school is close to where he works. The first two days were a nightmare. Wills didn't want to go. He refused to get out of bed, then shut himself in the bathroom, then said they would have to make him go naked because he wasn't going to get dressed. But his protests didn't last long, even though I knew from his frequent text messages that he had struggled at first. He said he was in a class of donkeys who hadn't got a clue how to behave themselves. He said that even I was brighter than most of them (thanks for the compliment), and that even I was better at basketball than most of them (thanks again). He complained about the food as well, saying that it was all that healthy rubbish that wussies like.

Dad brings Wills back home again in the evening. I was amazed that he had agreed to do it, but I guessed he was just trying to do his bit like everyone else. I was a bit jealous at first, because it meant that Wills got to see more of Dad than I did, but I couldn't really complain since I had Mum to myself more often than Wills did.

Wills has been picked for the school basketball team and he now has matches on a Saturday afternoon. Dad takes him to those as well and stays to support him. Suddenly, I seem to have so much time and so much space and it's SO QUIET. I can watch the sport on the telly and see every goal and every try and every wicket and every run. I can play race games, and it's not so bad losing to computer-generated bikes. I can disappear up to my room and do some reading or writing without being disturbed.

But I still like going to the library. I was so glad that Penny still wanted me to go there, and that she hasn't lumped me together with Wills because of what has happened.

'How's life with less of Wills?' she asked me

when I went in there for the first time after Wills had changed schools.

'Dull,' I chuckled, 'but it's nice to have Mum to myself sometimes. And I've got more time for reading, so I'll need to borrow more books.'

'You'll have more time for writing as well,' said Penny.

'It's so hard to know what to write about.'

'If all else fails,' she said, 'write about yourself.'

'That would be the most boring story ever,' I frowned.

'You'd be surprised,' Penny argued. 'Don't you put yourself down, young man. You leave that to Wills.'

As soon as I was fit enough again, I began to stay after school to play football, since I didn't have to get home early to keep an eye on Wills. I even go to play at the scrapyard. Everyone wanted me to tell them every gory detail of what had happened there. The door of the building has been boarded up again, but the boys press against it, hoping to be able to peer through and see the hole in the ceiling. It made me feel like a bit of a celebrity, until Jack brought me down to earth with a bump by saying I was a dolt to go in there in the first place.

Some weekends, if Wills doesn't have a basketball match, he stays at home to spend time with Mum and I go to Dad's on my own. We sit in his cocoon and shout at the telly together, not so loud that there's a thumping on the ceiling, but loud enough to make us feel that we are there in the crowd at the match. We clean his car together, then go to the park to kick a ball around, and I'm careful not to bowl him over. I haven't been back to basketball on Sunday mornings. I don't want to. I'd only gone in the first place because of Wills. There's no need any more, and I was never going to be better than average. Besides, I couldn't bear to see the other boys in the team again. They would lump me together with Wills, I am sure of it, so I would always be blamed for losing the tournament.

Wills went on a school trip for a week, the first

time a school had ever agreed to take him. It was some sort of outward bound thing, and I didn't envy him at all. The house was so unbelievably quiet that it got to the point where I couldn't wait to have Wills back. Mum spent the week on tenterhooks, waiting for the telephone call that would mean she had to bring him home early.

The telephone call didn't come and at the end of the week Dad went to collect him. When we heard the car drive up, Mum and I rushed to the front door and waved. Wills charged up the path, swung Mum round in a big circle, punched me in the arm, and demanded, 'What's to eat, Mum? I'm starving,' before running into the kitchen and raiding the fridge.

Dad stood on the front doorstep, beads of sweat pooling on his forehead.

'Would you like a cup of tea?' Mum smiled.

'I could murder one,' puffed Dad.

Wills had already plonked himself in front of the telly, volume LOUD, leaving a trail of empty packets all across Mum's nice clean kitchen. I sat down next to him.

'What was it like?' I asked.

'It was all right,' he said, spraying me with muffin. 'There was an assault course that would have made you wet yourself if you had had to go on it, but I was the best. Mum, can we have pizza tonight, please, Mumsy-wumsy?'

'As a special treat, yes,' said Mum, 'but no Coke.' She gave him a big hug. 'It's good to see you, Wills.'

'Good to see you too, Mum. Have you missed me?'

'We've all missed you, Wills.'

'I bet Chrissy-wissy hasn't.'

'It's been great,' I said. 'Best time of my life.'

Wills leapt on top of me. 'Take that back,' he growled, 'or I'll tickle you to death.'

'I take it back, I take it back,' I screamed as he began to tickle me mercilessly.

'I've got a surprise for you,' Dad said then. 'Sit still and I'll show you.'

We sat still while he delved into his pocket. He pulled out three tickets and waved them in the air. 'Motor racing, tomorrow. Are you coming?'

'You bet!' we cried.

'Well done, Wills,' he said. 'The first report from your school was really good, so you deserve a reward.'

I ignored the fact that, even though my reports were always good, I had never had a reward. I was pleased for Wills and I was pleased that for once Dad had kept a promise. Wills began to run round the room, making racing-car noises. Mum put her fingers in her ears, and Dad said it was time for him to go. 'NYEEEEAHHH, NYEEEAHHH, NYEEEAHHH,' went Wills, until Mum yelled at the top of her voice, 'STOP IT, WILLIAM, NOW!'

Wills stopped in his tracks, sat down on the settee, and grinned sheepishly at Mum. 'Sorry, Mum,' he said.

I went upstairs, saying I wanted an early night.

I sat down at my desk and pulled out a sheet of paper.

HURRICANE WILLS, I wrote, BY CHRIS JENNINGS.

What a great title, I thought. I would use the

same beginning as before, if I could remember it. I would write a lot of the same things as before. But the story wouldn't really be about Wills. NO WAY JOSE. It would be about ME.

I put the sheet under some other papers and got ready for bed. I would write my story, no matter how long it took, no matter how old I was by the time I finished it. I would write my story.

YEH!